THE MISSING TENANT

A Veronica Pilchard Mystery

ROZ GOLDIE

Copyright © 2015 Roz Goldie

All rights reserved, including the right to reproduce this book, or portions thereof in any form. No part of this text may be reproduced, transmitted, downloaded, decompiled, reverse engineered, or stored, in any form or introduced into any information storage and retrieval system, in any form or by any means, whether electronic or mechanical without the express written permission of the author.

This is a work of fiction. Names and characters are the product of the author's imagination and any resemblance to actual persons, living or dead, is entirely coincidental.

The views expressed in this work are solely those of the author and do not necessarily reflect the views of the publisher, and the publisher hereby disclaims any responsibility for them.

ISBN: 978-1-326-42933-1

PublishNation, London
www.publishnation.co.uk

Printed by Henderson Print

For Smartypants

Introduction

A middle aged woman lay in bed in the bright light of the Intensive Care Unit, in a medically induced coma. Nurses were working with a patient in the adjoining bed as a tall man with a thick brown mop of hair and a purposeful stride approached and silently took a seat beside her bed. When one of the staff recognised him and smiled he nodded. After three days all the nursing staff knew DI Jack Summers.

"No real change I'm afraid, Jack." The taller nurse said. "You can see from the chart."

The plain clothes policeman grunted a muted thank you and lifted the chart clipped to the end of the metal bedframe. He studied the information, or at least as much of it as he could understand and replacing the clip board to its usual resting place, he turned to the woman lying as if in a deep sleep.

"Veronica Pilchard, you have really ripped the ass out of it this time." He voice was lowered and his furrowed brown showed great anxiety.

The woman stirred, groaning slightly. He looked into her face as she opened her eyes, blinking in bright clinical space.

"Veronica! Are you going to wake up?" Jack choked on the words with obvious emotion.

A nurse quickly appeared at his side, pushing him out of her path, firmly but politely whispering "Excuse me." She pressed a button on the headboard of the bed, summonsing a doctor.

Jack shot to his feet, stepped back and stood to attention.

An elderly man in a white coat came into the ward. "Curtains please Nurse." He turned to Jack, "You will have to wait outside. We have some work to do."

And so Veronica Pilchard came back from the edge of brain death and was speaking to Jack Summers within a couple of hours.

The events leading up to that seemingly miraculous recovery were known to DI Summers and the police at Donaghdubh station. Jack Summers was one of the few who had genuine concern and sympathy for Veronica Pilchard. Most of the officers thought she had brought this misfortune upon herself and should never have been undertaking what was police business, and investigating serious crime with her amateur sleuthing.

Veronica's first coherent words were "I am very hungry. Can I have something to eat?"

The nurse laughed. "That one's a fighter!" Turning to Veronica she grinned, "We will get you as much as you are allowed to eat – promise."

* * * * *

Out of intensive care Veronica had a bed by the window on the fifth floor of the hospital. Beside her bed lay a small pile of cards – as yet unopened. These had been sent by the people now central to Veronica's life. None arrived from her former social circle which was predictable enough. Veronica had closed down all contact with the tennis club and the couples she had once befriended as a married woman. These days her closest friend was Lady Margaret Beightin and her regular acquaintances were the people with whom she worked – as an independent producer, at the BBC radio station – and the gay community at the Golden Palace.

Still suffering from acute headache and multiple bruising, but happy to have been given a second meal she opened the cards carefully. The first thick cream vellum envelope contained a card with a reproduction of a Pre-Raphaelite painting – the Lady of Shallot – and read, "Dearest VP if you are reading this then you have pulled through, thank God. Best Margaret."

The largest card was from the set at the Golden Palace. It was a massive explosion of pink and silver flowers with tiny satin ribbon bows, and read, "Veronica sweetie, we all love you!!" Under this there were small personal messages from at least a dozen gay men, including her hairdresser Desmond Charles.

Barry Doyle had sent a card sporting a French Impressionist picture of a woman stooped over gathering in the harvest. His message was "Veronica I need my production woman working in the field – so get well soon." She laughed, knowing Barry would be as sentimental as anyone from the Golden Palace but would reserve any show of that for when they met in person – and far from the hospital. Barry had always hated hospitals, and even more so since his partner had died slowly in such a place, some time ago.

The whole team from the Barry Doyle Show had sent individual cards – giving the false impression that Veronica Pilchard had a very wide range of friends and social contacts.

There was no card from Harry, her now probably about-to-be ex-husband, but he had perhaps not yet heard of her accident. Nor was there anything from her only living relative, her sister in England, which is why Jack had nominated himself as de facto next of kin.

Now that she was conscious, well fed and her pain was fairly well under control Veronica had space to reflect on the so-called accident.

After the space of only two years Derek Deakin had been released on licence and set about taking revenge on the amateur sleuth who had created his downfall. Police had gathered evidence that convicted him of crimes he had committed but, by a twist of fate, another foul deed of which he was in fact innocent. This had rankled with him. His hatred for Veronica Pilchard festered over his time in prison – so he happily drove her car over the edge of a steep embankment.

She could remember little other than seeing his demonic face, contorted in a seething grin as her vehicle lurched out of control and nosedived into oblivion.

His car had been caught on security camera and he was arrested soon after – showing signs of a psychotic breakdown.

Veronica left hospital after another three days, with nothing more to show for the attempted murder than a headache and a scar hidden by the hair brushed slightly over her cheek. She arrived home on a sweltering July afternoon – by taxi since her car was a write-off – and sat in the shade of the large apple tree in her back garden for some hours before rising look for food.

Although she would make a full recovery, physically, it took some time before she regained her customary pugnacious confidence. In the intervening weeks she divided her time between her production work for the Barry Dole show and her friend Margaret Beightin.

* * * * *

Chapter One

Veronica Pilchard had not seen much of her estranged husband since the April morning he'd arrived home unexpectedly and was met in his own hallway by an armed detective accosting him in the mistaken belief that he was an intruder with violent and criminal intent. The fact that Detective Inspector Jack Summers had emerged from upstairs, barely clothed and seemingly having an affair with his wife made Harry Pilchard angry, confused, humiliated and yet still somehow apprehensive. She had laughed at him and then asked to cook breakfast for them all!

Stunned by a reversal of marital infidelities Harry Pilchard was indignant – harbouring a lasting and dismal sense of betrayal. He had made a full Ulster fry for the policeman and his wife while he had sat, sulking, drinking only black coffee.

When DI Summers had left he turned to Veronica, "How could you?"

"I could have asked you that question on New Year's Eve but it seemed a rather fatuous question, Harry." Her voice was cold as she thought of how he was the one who had been serially unfaithful. "Anyway, dearest, I don't think this will turn out to be a grand romance."

Her amateur sleuthing had got results but had come with serious personal threat – which was why DI Summers had been armed when he confronted the apparent intruder.

* * * * *

That all seemed a long time ago as another autumn set in. Veronica Pilchard was now completely absorbed in her work with Barry Doyle, for her independent production company making the midday slot into a ratings booster for local BBC radio.

Although she'd been reluctant at first to even consider the possibility of working with him, Barry Doyle had changed since the times when he had poured scorn on her documentaries. Over the years in Dublin in Radio Turf he'd matured and after the death of his partner he returned to Belfast quite a different person. In a remarkable turnaround he had come to admire Veronica's approach to programme making. The two were still working on a short-term contracts – with high audience targets, exacting conditions and a strictly probationary agreement.

Noel Fitzpatrick had kept his staff job as head of department, turning down the offer to join Veronica's *Authenticity Productions*. His family commitments made that option too risky a move. He was, however, an old ally of Veronica's and likely to benefit considerably if the Barry Doyle Show continued to be as successful as expected.

Studio production was a daily treadmill that Veronica could avoid as a rule – unless there was a live discussion with serious legal implications. In that case she would be there in person and occasionally with legal support. Today she had the opportunity to lie in bed as long as she wanted as her work was done for the next few days and Barry Doyle was more than happy with the features on which they had collaborated.

Today, however, was the deadline for a decision about whether she and Harry were to sell the marital home in the village of Glenbannock where they'd lived for some years before separating. Harry had taken a number of contracts, the latest being to organise a national youth sporting tournament in England. Since that work was now coming to an end he was demanding a decision on two crucial issues – their marital status and whether or not their home was to be sold.

Veronica had prevaricated and kept herself sufficiently preoccupied so she could avoid thinking about either of these decisions and the implications it would have for the foreseeable future in terms of both her home and her marriage, if it could still be called that.

Unable to sustain this state of complete denial the need to come to some conclusion weighed heavily on her shoulders. It was with this indecision, and growing irritation that she got out of bed at half past six.

* * * * *

Veronica's friend and fellow sleuth Margaret Beightin was not around to give her the advice and direction that was usually on hand – alongside the encouragement she sorely needed that morning. Lady Beightin was on a three-week cruise and was not due back for another fortnight. It did not occur to her to contact Jack Summers. The distance from Margaret bothered her more than she would readily admit since Veronica Pilchard was too proud to concede any sort of dependency.

Downstairs sitting with strong black coffee and her first cigarette of the day she considered her options. There was not much hope that she and Harry would get back together again. In all probability the house would have to be sold. She could rent an apartment in Belfast before house-hunting. That would be convenient for her work.

The thought of getting the house into shape for viewing was depressing – she loathed housework and would have to pack away a lot of her everyday working materials. Suddenly the easy life of the temporary singleton she'd been enjoying for held no attraction. The prospect of living in permanent solitude was rather daunting for a woman who was turning fifty. Her new acquaintances were on the gay scene, introduced to her by Barry Doyle, and always pleasant but not really close friends. She had become isolated from her usual social circle, and quite deliberately so – after the colossal humiliation and embarrassment that came with the public revelation that Harry had been having affairs with a considerable number of women over the years. Since that New Year's Eve debacle she had not set foot in the tennis club or contacted their mutual friends.

Biting back tears, Veronica acknowledged for just a moment that she was frightened. Then she gulped down the last of coffee, stood to attention and headed straight for her workroom.

She started into sorting out the things she needed on a daily basis – remarkably little once she had piled up her lap-top, recorder and contacts book. Much of the remainder was information which was either out of date or available from other sources. So she began to declutter her entire office, finishing the job in three hours. It would take some time to shred any potentially confidential reports but she felt a rush of energy and confidence when she stood back to inspect the heap of extraneous items that had encumbered her for the past few years. She was elated by a sense of freedom. She simply didn't need most of that stuff!

Quite irrationally she equated this sense of release with her relationship with Harry. If the house had to be sold then the matter was settled. Veronica decided that before the day was out she would dump the unwanted things from her office and shred anything else about which she had reservations.

Before that she would have another coffee, a smoke and look on line for city-centre apartments. However, finding apartments in Belfast in September meant competing with a large population of students as the academic year began in colleges and universities.

* * * * *

Harry Pilchard had succeeded in making the youth sports tournament a great success and had managed to achieve a high media profile. He was now in demand across the whole sector – meaning that he could pick his work and name his price. This did a great deal to enhance his self-esteem. Now that he was about to return to Glenbannock he realised that Veronica had not occupied his thoughts a great deal, once the sting of indignity at being cuckolded had worn off. In truth he missed the domesticity and the stability of village life, cooking and the continuity of being in his own home more than he missed his wife. Living in hotels and rented accommodation meant that he had very little equipment for proper cooking. He had only made a big issue of selling the house to annoy Veronica but he firmly intended to stay there – even if he had to buy her out.

Today was the decision deadline he'd imposed on her while still very angry with her infidelity. Now, as he sat at breakfast, he looked over the calculations he had made some months before. He'd made astute investments in the past and now that the market was more buoyant he could make a tidy profit. That would more than cover half the price of their house – his home. Harry Pilchard had every intention of staying in Glenbannock.

He had made up his mind to take a few weeks off, settle back home and then return to events management on short contracts. He was a happy and confident man – whether or not he would remain a married one.

* * * * *

Wild Fern Alley was well known in the University area, having been the first local scheme where residents had managed to get the Council to gate off the Alleyway and then set about planting wild herbs and flowers, making seats and painting back walls, doors and fences. It had gone from being a site for underage prostitution and nightly drug dealing to a place of peace and tranquillity for residents. A key person among that select community was a strong-minded woman who was a theatrical landlady and former actress by the name of Marianne Kelly. A lady of a certain age Marianne sported a thick head of luscious auburn hair that swirled around her finely boned face and straight shoulders. She had the poise of someone who had trained in dancing and spoke with a musical tone of voice.

Bertie Norton knew her and suggested that Veronica might like to begin her newly enforced nomadic life by staying there for a short while.

"She is a star, my dear!" Bertie trilled in obvious admiration. "I can't tell you how many people I know have stayed with her!" He smiled knowingly. "And here's her card."

Veronica was attempting to keep up the appearance of equanimity, fighting back a menacing sense of an unknown future as she sat in the epicentre of the gay social scene, the Golden Palace with Bertie and Barry Doyle. Harry had come home in defiant mood and told her in no uncertain manner that he was not selling the house and the choice was hers.

"Stay with me or leave – that's your decision. If you are leaving I will buy out your share of the house." His voice was cold, aloof and approaching the punitive.

"Well, damn you, Harry!" Veronica had been taken completely by surprise. He was making no effort to repair their relationship and seemed to enjoy being in control – in control of his life, without regard to her. Stung to the quick she retorted, "Then buy me out!"

"Fine! And when you do go I can get the place fumigated so that the smell of your filthy cigarettes stops clinging to the very fabric of the house!"

There were no tears shed – on either side – since Veronica's pride forbade any admission to the depth of the pain she was experiencing and Harry felt vindicated after her demeaning him by being unfaithful – not pausing to remind himself that he was the serial womaniser and she had been a faithful wife for all those years. Harry Pilchard never entirely recovered from being two-timed by an armed policeman in his own home!

Some premonition must have motivated Veronica as, before his return, she had cleared her office leaving a bare minimum of equipment and had sorted out her other belongings – many of which went to charity shops over that week. She was, in fact, in a position where she could have loaded her worldly goods into the car that night. She chose not to do so.

The following day she had cracked after the Barry Doyle show, in the privacy of the production office – where Barry had given her a shoulder to cry on.

"Veronica, if that's how he is behaving you should move out." He handed her another paper tissue. "He wouldn't get violent, would he?"

"God no!" She laughed and blew her nose. "He isn't that sort of man – I'd never put up with that!"

"Let's go to the Golden Palace for a bite of lunch and talk it over where we have friends. You know Bertie will never forget you collaring that beast who beat the hell out of him."

Veronica was too grateful to say that the Golden Palace was not a place where she had a lot of friends, or that she didn't actually have a lot of friends –now that she had left the social circle where she and Harry had been a settled perfect couple for so many years.

"Thanks Barry. That would be nice."

"What about your policeman friend?"

"Oh Jack? I haven't seen a lot of him – that was just a fling, on both sides really."

"But it was fun wasn't it sweetie?" Barry teased.

And so it was Barry's friend Bertie Norton who eased Veronica's passage into Marianne Kelly's guest house for thespians and Wild Fern Alley.

* * * * *

"Of course there are still some rowdy drunken students but things have calmed down a lot recently." Marianne made conversation easily as she sat with Veronica in the large kitchen. "A room at the back would be quieter for you." She poured two cups of coffee and pushed a ceramic ashtray in front of her new guest. "You look like you need a smoke. Don't use them any more myself but I do remember."

"Thank God you are not the pious sort of reformed smoker!" She did not add, like my about- to-be ex-husband.

"Yes some people get very sniffy don't they?" She smiled. "We prefer people to smoke in what we now call the designated area – and not in the bedrooms."

"And this is designated space?" Veronica was clearly wondering about whether smoking could possibly be permitted in the kitchen.

"No, but we've just met and I'd like us to get along. The official area is in the old study. It has been extended with a sun room into the garden." She pointed towards the modern extension on the back of the house.

Having shown her a well-furnished en-suite bedroom, which Veronica admired greatly, Marianne was about to leave her to find her bearings and decide whether she wanted to stay.

"When is the room free?" Veronica was eager to move out of Glenbannock as soon as humanly possible.

"It's free now." Marianne gave her a ring with keys to the front door and her room.

"Thank you, Marianne. If possible I'd like to take it tonight for a month."

"Grand. You have the keys so come and go as you please." She held out her hand to shake on the deal.

Veronica was not sure if she would even stay for as long as a month but wanted to secure a bed for at least that amount of time. Circumstances were to affect her plans as the neighbourhood around Wild Fern Alley was to see a mysterious series of crimes. For the moment Marianne's house was the base from which she would work. Veronica Pilchard moved in that afternoon, complete with her meagre collection of clothes and personal possessions.

* * * * *

Marianne Kelly was central to a local residents' group who had formed a community collective of professionals and retired people who lived in the homes backing onto Wild Fern Alley. Although it had taken some years to get permission to gate off the alleyway the group had formed solid and increasingly trusting relationships – despite having very different political, cultural and sexual preferences.

As far as officials in the Council and various government departments were concerned the two main characters were Marianne and Thaddeus James, since they were the named people who sought authorisations – and occasionally sought forgiveness having acted before getting permission. Thaddeus James was a retired law professor who had taken to painting after a lifetime of excellence in academia. He was the group's unofficial legal advisor. More importantly he was their horticultural mentor as few of the neighbours had experience of successful gardening.

Over several years they had met with resistance from property owners in the district who saw themselves as custodians of the area, regardless of the fact they flouted planning restrictions. Wild Fern Alley was enveloped by residences that had once been family homes but which had been turned in houses of multiple occupation – and the occupants were usually students and frequently anti-social. As property prices and rents had increased these local landlords had become millionaires and now considered themselves to be people of substance – to the point of joining, supporting and buying their way up the hierarchy of various and even opposing political parties.

As property magnates they felt justified in acting as a private vigilante force, gently but firmly undermining community development and collective activity in the area. There were few communal spheres that they considered as being off-limits – among which were the Buddhist Centre and the Local Church. Of the five men who owned some eight hundred properties Brendan Cobbles and Shappie McVeigh were the most vociferous. Thaddeus was a quiet man in his late seventies who tended to avoid confrontation and kept a low profile. Marianne was more prominent and likely to speak her mind when the occasion arose. Her customary sophisticated and gracious manner gave her a quiet authority which Councillor Cobbles disliked and deeply envied.

Cobbles had only just managed to squeeze into power by a slim majority in the local Council elections – so slim he was in danger of losing his seat at the next ballot. However, he was now a public representative and was to be seen on a daily basis patrolling the surrounding streets consorting with the few who were his equal. From the great heights of his social advancement and individual wealth he looked down on the local residents and intensely distrusted their motives for mutual improvement and co-operative action. He and Shappie McVeigh infiltrated local groups, attended their meetings and studied the potential for disrupting developments such as Wild Fern Alley – this followed a pattern of years. Frederick Stewart was another local landlord, though his priority was his art gallery.

Despite the landlords' efforts, once the gates were up and locked the residents worked well among themselves and with those nominated by the university to improved public relations and the image of their students. The university donated large amounts of compost and a variety of plants. Environmental health operatives took away the debris amassed over years and collected by residents over the weeks and produced a series of recycling containers. Neighbours offered help to those who could not decorate or garden. Children and grandchildren were recruited to paint back doors, stencil on red brick and grey walls and refurbish seating areas.

Within weeks the space was transformed. Local landlords were unhappy and suspiciously watched these enhancements.

* * * * *

The Golden Palace was the centre of night life for the gay community in Belfast and the hub of their social networks. That was where a person could hear gossip, rumour and information that had not yet made the news and some information that never would get into the public arena. And that was where Veronica had stumbled upon a vital link to the perpetrators of murder and child abuse, which she had passed on to the police two years previously. Nowadays she went there to meet people with stories or introductions to those who would talk to Barry Doyle for the daily show.

As often as not she'd meet Bertie Norton a waiter at the exclusive and expensive Merchant Studio restaurant. He was always an enthusiastic informant, grateful for her part in convicting the sadistic predatory homosexual Deakin who had assaulted him – and even more so after the attack on Veronica.

And the Golden Palace regularly served as the unofficial production office for the Barry Doyle Show.

That evening she had walked into the city centre enjoying the pleasant September weather. As she got to the Golden Palace she met her hairdresser, Desmond, from *Curl up and Dye*.

"Ah Veronica, crossing to the other side again!" He teased her as one of the few straight people who was a regular.

"Essential networking, Desmond." She smiled. Desmond had become fond of her since meeting her in his own social clique. She was more than a customer now.

"So are you on the prowl tonight?" She asked, knowing that Desmond was a notorious flirt and rarely formed lasting relationships.

"My dear! I never do prowling – purring perhaps but never prowling."

Barry Doyle had smoothed her path into the social scene at the Golden Palace so that she was now accepted as a trustworthy confidante.

Veronica whispered theatrically "There is a very nice young man who is staying with Marianne and I thought he'd like it here. I gave him the address and directions, so keep an eye out."

* * * * *

Leaving home life in Glenbannock had been a relief to Veronica once Harry had installed himself back home. Petty irritations such as her smoking and lack of interest in creature comforts had become the source of his exasperation and then anger – even before a full day had elapsed. Veronica did not pause to consider whether there was more to his moodiness than their now-inevitable divorce. His easy charm simply evaporated in her presence. He snapped at her on numerous occasions during her last morning in the house and so she upped and left as soon as the opportunity arose. Harry was a changed man but she was not to discover why for some time to come. Freed from the sense of foreboding in what had once been her home, she drove to Belfast enjoying a definite feeling of emancipation.

Belfast offered easy access to most of the things that interested her. She could walk into the city centre in fifteen minutes and enjoyed the exercise. Oblivious to the smell of petrol fumes Veronica was glad to be far from the stench of slurry spraying. Far from the fields of crops and profusion of weeds her hay fever would surely disappear within days. Even the wild ferns that graced the alley, among the well pruned herbs and geraniums, could not diminish its attractions. Life in the home of a quiet, unpretentious but clearly talented landlady would surely provide a pleasant routine. Unlike Harry, Marianne had shown genuine interest in her work from the very beginning of the friendship and even made some suggestions about programme ideas. Thus the first two weeks passed as a pleasant, stress-free experience – to such an extent that Veronica felt that this change was not to be feared but rather an alternative and better way of living.

Although there was a strong community in the area, life under the shadow of Queen's University was utterly devoid of the village parochialism and somehow the gossip appeared to a somewhat gullible Veronica as less malign.

In that first fortnight Veronica became involved in the life of the Alley and local folk during her few free evenings. She went so far as to resume an old habit of knitting – as the Alley was about to be festooned with brightly coloured woollen swags on lampposts and street furniture. This was 'yarn bombing' which was a practice originating from the response of an arts based collective to the uninvited erection union flags and painting of curb stones to curtain and carpet public spaces – thus marking out territory controlled by so-called 'locals' aided if not armed by paramilitary factions.

"Oh, we did a lot of that last summer – Bogtown Road had become a sea of red white and blue overnight and you can imagine how a lot of Catholic residents felt about that." Marianne spoke with assertion but no animosity. "It started on Facebook and took off quickly."

Veronica did not participate in any social media networks. She gave a non-committal nod, and asked. "Is this new – Carpeting Bogtown Road with flags?"

"It used to be a neutral space because Catholics, Protestants and people of other religions and none live there in a friendly community. The mass of huge flags is to mark the territory and defy any show of tolerance." She flipped open her phone and showed Veronica some pictures. "As you see some people have used brightly coloured scarves and fabrics, as well as the knitted collars. It somehow makes the area seem much less hostile. Anyway we decided to do the same in Wild Fern Alley. If you can knit that would be appreciated."

"If you have needles I can get some wool and give it a try." Veronica was not going to boast about her skill at knitting. Nor was she going to admit the warm feeling of acceptance that she felt.

"Oh there's a community wool bank – you don't have to buy anything." Marianne said happily. "Anything you could do would be welcome. You know not many people can knit these days."

To her surprise Veronica still found the dull repetition of knitting plain squares generated a sense of peace, order and security – and that while it kept her hands busy it freed her mind to wander in creative and unusual directions. Over those two weeks she produced a series of squares in primary colours, and in that process jotted down some of the most interesting ideas that had occurred to her as she stitched her evenings away in the sun room.

* * * * *

Eliza Taunter was Marianne's nearest neighbour and a professor of some 'ology' or other. Eliza made sure that people were aware of her academic status, whatever the setting. She attended community meetings about parking, and recycling bin collections but somehow managed to avoid doing anything of practical use.

Her usual excuse for refusing to take action or responsibility for things communal was, "I simply don't have the time!" Professor Taunter was always on her way to a conference, due at a book launch on her specialist subject – the science of words and symbols – or preparing a particularly abstruse journal paper. Marianne would listen patiently at meetings as the Professor detailed her important commitments, pausing occasionally to complain of slow progress on the latest community concern.

Happily for the others in the residents' informal association Eliza would inevitably have some reason to leave within half an hour. It was exactly this performance that the Professor enacted on the evening they met in the old study and sun room in Marianne's home.

"I am writing about the discursive inconsistencies in the debate about flags at Belfast City Hall." Eliza bowed her head slightly, her spectacles balanced half way down her thin nose, as if to emphasize the gravity of discursive inconsistency and the huge significance of her scholarly analysis. "I feel that dispute had been entirely misunderstood and that my deliberations will clarify matters."

Veronica sat knitting, listening and watching this routine with a mischievous interest that was rather too near to malice. This woman was a complete caricature of an academic! Discursive inconsistency? Of course politicians indulged in double-speak – that's how they manage their votes! She watched the reaction of the assembled group of eleven solid citizens noticing the discreet raising of eyebrows and not a sound other than a few mumbled coughs. The woman was as subtle as a pantomime horse Veronica thought, without seeing that this was precisely the same as the dynamics of communal meetings in villages like Glenbannock.

As an experienced radio producer Veronica knew the perils of interviewing the scholarly expert on any subject. Aside of some few and notable exceptions all academics gave a lecture – generally a meandering one – which would require a huge amount of editing. Her usual tactic was to wait until the scenario had been fully acted out and then repeat the initial, basic question in a little more detail. This usually elicited a short if condescending response which was all she would use for the planned feature or programme. From this experience she had created a virtual black list of worthy persons who claimed expertise but could not speak for less than twenty minutes on their given topic. She amused herself thinking of what Barry Doyle would do with Professor Eliza Taunton in the hot seat, live on air. She would ask him if he'd do a demolition job on her discursive inconsistencies.

The atmosphere lightened immediately Eliza left the room, – although no-one explicitly commented. Veronica was reminded of the honest country woman Martha McCoubrey who had observed that if she lived in a village she would have to learn to rub along with people whether or not they were to her taste. Veronica was not the sort to put her judgements to one side and 'rub along' and certainly not with a woman who had addressed her, sneeringly, as Marianne's new reporter.

The only way that she would convince Barry Doyle to have Eliza on the show to discuss the running sore that was the dispute over how many days the Union flag should fly was to make it enormously funny. She was sure that could be done. She knitted in the undeniable knowledge that she was nearer to Madame Lafarge sitting under the shadow of the guillotine than the benevolent Miss Marple of St Mary Mead.

* * * * *

Wild Fern Alley could be accessed from the back of houses along three streets. Detached houses on Montague Avenue ran at right angles to those on College Road and Crusaders' Lane. Veronica was surprised to discover that she already knew a number of local residents. Desmond Charles, her highly esteemed hairdresser, lived in Crusaders' Lane, as did Bertie Norton. She was about to discover that Detective Inspector Jack Summers had now taken up temporary residence in College Road in a large family house adjacent to a block of apartments in which her favourite audio engineer Andrew Simpson lived.

She had been sitting by her window looking into the Alley admiring her handiwork – now draped on lampposts in the Alley – when she saw Jack Summers appear from a courtyard with a watering can, intent on reviving some wilted herbs.

Without thinking she opened the window and shouted out "Hiya, Jack!"

"The bold Veronica Pilchard!" He waved and smiled. "Are we now neighbours?"

"Only temporarily, Jack." She suddenly felt rather stupid. They'd had a fling and she really should have let it go at that.

"Me too. It's a long story. I could tell you. Fancy a drink?" He was charming and seemed sincere – whatever ulterior motives he may have been harbouring. "Not sleuthing again I hope?" His tone was roguish.

"Me? No. I'm working. I've moved out of Glenbannock and staying her for a short time."

"Then I am safe to ask you out!" He teased.

"Thanks a lot!" Veronica was pleased to be asked.

"Have you eaten?"

"No. I was going out anyway."

"Then why don't we go together! I'll pick you up in twenty minutes."

And so Veronica and Jack Summers met up again. Due to the conditions of his house insurance Jack's father had to have someone living in his home while he spent the summer in Italy. However, his usual house-sitter had mysteriously disappeared and so the dutiful son was now keeping the familial fort safe.

* * * * *

As they strolled happily towards the city centre they looked like long term friends or partners, at ease with each other. They reached the Italian restaurant within a few minutes and were seated by the window on arrival. As usual Veronica was very focused on eating and took up the menu without further conversation.

"I'm starving. What do you fancy on the menu?" She was making it clear that she prioritised eating over social niceties.

"Sea food and then the pasta special!" Jack beamed. "This is a great place and I eat here a lot. You won't be disappointed."

They ordered food as soon as the waiter arrived – which was promptly.

"And to drink sir?" The waiter was jovially formal, clearly knowing Jack.

"Cosa consiglia?" Jack asked for his suggestion.

"Verdicchio would be perfect."

Jack nodded with a smile and the waiter jotted down the choice and left immediately.

"I didn't know you spoke Italian. I am impressed Jack!" Veronica was somewhat taken aback, having thought of Jack as a slightly up-market plod.

"I speak a bit. My father always took us to Italy for holidays and a few phrases don't go amiss."

Ignoring this reminder of the fact that she was a poor judge of people Veronica opened up another line of conversation. "Who is it that usually keeps house when your father is away?" Veronica had been instantly curious and was taking the first opportunity to ask without appearing overly inquisitive.

"An Italian researcher who lives with students during the academic year. He gets a rent free billet for the summer. Has done for the past six years. My father trusts him so it's odd that he didn't show up as planned. He was only supposed to be away for a couple of days and that was a week ago." Jack was not immediately assuming something suspicious. "Anyway it happens to suit me as I have sold my place – it's far too big – and I'm house hunting or rather looking for anywhere smaller and cheaper to run." He did not say that he had hoped for a rapprochement with his ex-wife for some years and finally admitted that he was now completely if not permanently single.

"What's the researcher's name?"

"Nicola Tebaldi. He's from near Verona and is a post-doctoral Fellow in the School of Law." Jack looked at her guardedly. "I don't have his age, weight, height, blood group or hair colour." He teased.

"I didn't ask!" Veronica snapped.

The waiter arrived with a bottle of white wine, showing it to Jack for approval. He nodded his assent and the wine was duly opened and poured.

The two raised their glasses and made an unspoken toast before drinking.

Changing tack Jack began his own investigation. "Why are you staying with Marianne?"

"Harry gave me a choice – stay with him in his stinking temper or move. He's buying out my share of the house."

Jack guffawed. "I shouldn't laugh but I can't get the picture of Harry out of my head – standing in his own hallway with me threatening to shoot him!"

"I don't think he can get that picture out of his head either!" Her voice rang with less than light hearted humour. "He was determined to stay in Glenbannock and to get rid of me – I have been thinking about that but I have no idea why he had to be so vindictive. Harry isn't really like that."

"And you think you know what your partner is really like?" Jack cleared his throat, but said nothing more. Veronica was a lucky sleuth and great fun but she was such a lousy judge of character.

She drew a swift breath through her teeth, hissing as she did so, "I shall ignore that Jack."

The food arrived and Veronica immediately set to eating.

Conversation stopped as they munched their way through a large plate of seafood in a light vinaigrette.

"You were right Jack. I was not disappointed!" Veronica's mood had lightened considerably with that delicious first course but she still could not resist showing off her own minimal Italian. "Molto bene!"

"So you are no less competitive then?" Jack teased.

She put her hands up in a gesture of pacification if not submission "Sorry, could not pass up the chance."

He laughed and poured another glass of wine for them both.

"Actually, I have been thinking about following up on Nicola. You see he is very fond of my father and he is usually punctual to a fault. I have been working on a difficult case and I just let it go. Mind you I do think there must be a good reason for his going AWOL."

As the pasta had been set in front of them they let the subject lie and set about finishing the rest of their meal.

* * * * *

Despite the fact that the Northern Ireland peace process had been rumbling on for the many years since the Belfast Agreement, there were always contentious matters that drove the Unionist and Nationalist politicians and people into separate and bitterly opposed camps. Pro-union Orange Order marches were held in every part of the land were held by the thousand, passing off without rancour. However there were always a few of that were acrimoniously opposed by Nationalist residents and their representatives. There were also Nationalist and republican proposals for a museum of the conflict which angered Unionists as much as the welter of newly enacted equality and human rights legislation that underpinned the peace agreement. In recent years one of the most virulent disputes arose around the flying of the Union flag. The union jack as it is called locally has a long history of controversy in Northern Ireland as far back as the late 1940s and again in 1953 with the Queen's coronation, when nationalist Councils refused to display British flags and emblems. This led the Stormont government to enact law banning the symbolic expression of any form of Irish nationalism. Even the 1987 repeal left things ambiguous as it did not settle debates on the symbols of sovereignty, the Union Flag and the Irish Tricolour. The peace agreement did no better for the simple reason that no compromise could be found despite the byzantine machinations of civil servants and negotiators. Summer 2000 saw a partial solution when it was agreed to end the habit of flying the union jack every day of the year on government buildings. A new set of agreed days – designated days like the Queen's birthday – would be set aside for flying the British Flag.

To anyone outside Northern Ireland the debate about Irish and or British flags appeared to be childish, and a petulant and vindictive performance of staged political opposition. Still, inside Northern Ireland the debate raged on as the political landscape changed and Nationalist and Republicans took their democratic place in government and local councils. The chamber in Belfast Council changed political colours from Unionist orange to Nationalist green. Where Unionists had once held total control Nationalists and Republican were close to taking the reins of power.

Veronica had watched this with interest and also frustration as the years went by. She had a rough idea of what had led to the dispute but she had not felt the slightest need to examine the issue in forensic detail – until Eliza Taunter got under her skin, reviving in her an avid if not spiteful competitiveness.

She laid aside her knitting needles and took to the internet in search of some detail – finding to her amazement, and dismay, that there were a vast number of sites dedicated to the subject. She determined to mine these for accurate reports on these events. Before embarking on a very long night of research she looked up the profile and publications that Eliza Taunter had uploaded to the stratosphere of social media.

"Jesus! This calls for a stiff drink." Veronica was so horrified by the language and obscurity of the material that she saved a couple of files and closed down the computer. She decided against the strong drink and went out in the evening glow, walking towards the river and parklands. Her head was swimming with the incomprehensible terminology, unintelligible references and the huge number of footnotes.

She walked briskly running her hands through her hair at the back of her neck, as if the action would disentangle her brain cells. She breathed deeply taking in the soft air, and shrugged her shoulders several times. Reaching the embankment Veronica remembered walking there, hand in hand with Harry in the early days of their romance. Now the trees and shrubs had grown considerably and filled most of the green space between the pavement and the water. The Lagan itself had been dredged a number of times since then so that it was no longer the stinking morass at low tide. Here the sky was wide, open and generous. She was already missing the rural skies of Glenbannock. The gestation of her divorce had been over two years and she pondered on whether she was actually missing Harry, deciding that the very question answered itself.

"Veronica!" A voice called out from behind her.

She swung round to see Desmond, waving and smiling. "Desmond. How nice to see you. Are you taking your constitutional?"

"Yes, I always take a walk at this time unless I have something better on offer." He laughed. "And is this your normal haunt?"

"No, I'm not much of a walker. I just needed to clear my head – I've been trying to read some stuff that Eliza Taunter wrote. It's done my head in, I can tell you!"

"Ah, the professor of fuck-all-ogy!" Desmond spat the words out in obvious disgust. "Veronica you really should know better."

"What do you mean? Have you some gossip? Oh please do share!" She grinned broadly, relieved that there was a possibility that the odious Eliza was actually a fraud and not a high brow scholar.

"Well" Desmond drawled, lengthening the word for theatrical purposes. "She puts herself about as if she is a world famous academic but she's a real bitch and I've heard she stole a lot of her material!"

"You know somebody she has really pissed off! Tell all Desmond, pleeeease!" Veronica felt a spiteful pleasure and righteous indignation as well as a genuine curiosity, and would milk every detail from her hairdresser.

"My new junior, Sandy. He's one of her students and was doing well until she failed him on his assignments. She told him he should stick to trichology – that's hairdressing – and he told her she was the queen of trick-ology. The cow reported him and now he's up on a disciplinary!"

"That's a bit steep. Is the lad any good as a student?"

"He's a straight A student – though he's not straight of course." Desmond tittered. "He was doing fine until he took her module. The problem with Sandy is that he's clever and very independent, so he disagreed with her in tutorial and she exploded!"

"In this day and age, with the amount students pay I'd think he could appeal that. Anyway what about this idea that she steals other people's work? Is there any evidence of that?" Veronica had an unwholesome interest.

"There were rumours at the McClintock Institute – where she was before – but nothing solid. That was until Sandy met a guy from McClintock."

"You're not just being protective of your protégé Desmond?"

"Oh, no my dear. Sandy's friend had the bad luck to have her as a supervisor and she ripped off a lot of his fieldwork – but she didn't really understand the finer points and seriously misinterpreted it." Desmond was standing bolt upright, shoulders straight and gesturing with his hands, semaphore-like, in the manner of an old fashioned opera singer. "At least that's what Nicola told Sandy."

"Nicola? Would that be Nicola Tebaldi by any chance?"

"How could you possibly know that?" Desmond was flabbergasted.

"Just a coincidence." Veronica was thinking about the missing tenant and the possibility that Desmond's protégé might have some information. "Tell me Desmond, is Sandy working at your place tomorrow?"

"Yes, he should be in after lunch. Are you onto another of your mysteries Veronica?" He was cautiously apprehensive, recalling the scar on her head that he had skillfully disguised with a special haircut.

"No it's just that a friend of mine was expecting Nicola to house-sit for his father for the rest of the month but he hasn't shown up for a week." She would have to tell Jack Summers but first she would talk to Sandy. "I'll call in tomorrow afternoon – might even take up some of your time if you're not too busy!" She tried to sound less agitated than her instinct dictated.

"I'll shift another client if needs be – I always have time for you. As long as you don't repeat the do-it-yourself hair dye!" Desmond laughed as he recollected the hijab-clad Veronica appearing for emergency treatment, tearfully admitting to her disastrous attempts at colouring her hair.

"Thank you." Veronica was still unable to see the funny side of that escapade. "Well, I must get back to my computer – and thanks it will be less daunting to look at the trick-ologist's work now."

They parted ways and Veronica retraced her steps back from the broad reaches of the embankment through the narrow streets of the Holyland up Damascus Street towards the larger houses and Marianne's establishment. Night was falling and the first arrivals of the new semester's intake of students were beginning a round of noisy drunken parties. She walked purposefully past the open-air celebrations, noisy music and Irish tricolours fluttering out windows, thinking of this was a blatant disregard for people who lived locally – and no better than the sea of union flags on Bogtown road.

As she closed the large front doors behind her Veronica felt safer. The atmosphere changed as it grew dark and the territory was taken over by young people who marked their ground with noise, symbols and an underlying belligerence.

"Ah you have seen some of our new residents." Marianne said. "They are not as bad as they seem. And there are not so many now. Though that's because there is a better market with young professionals who can't afford to buy!" Her tone did not hide her contempt for the landlords.

Veronica accepted the invitation to coffee in the kitchen, knowing she had a long night ahead of research and could use the caffeine buzz.

* * * * *

It was cold in the basement. Nicola had a light jacket and there was only one dirty blanket on the mattress. He was not certain how he had got there but felt sure he knew where he was – in Eliza Taunter's basement with no more than the light from a small filthy window that looked onto a red brick wall. His phone was gone and his watch. His only way of judging time was by the amount of light outside. He reckoned it was nine or so as darkness was falling.

The faint noises outside could have come from any number of activities but he guessed that it was the sound of students celebrating before the onset of the new academic year in their now-traditional way.

Nicola was more confused than frightened. He understood that he had been abducted but did not know why he was now imprisoned.

There was neither sound nor heat from the house above. Reluctantly he pulled the blanket over himself and waited patiently.

* * * * *

Before returning to her computer Veronica made a note of her conversation with Desmond in her usual untidy scrawl adding arrows to the names Jack and Eliza Taunter. She put her notebook to one side and returned to the internet and reports of the flags dispute.

She quickly got a picture of the political developments leading up to the current quarrel. After the Belfast Agreement the Belfast Council Chamber no longer witnessed the fist fights of the 1970s and 1980s. The balance of power went from a Unionist domination to Nationalist and Republican holding sway and the colour went from orange to green, with a realisation that working relationships had to be built and sustained – but not always in the public eye. Where once the city had been ruled by those loyal to the Crown times had changed.

In 2005 the Council was embroiled in a heated debate over funding the St Patrick's Day Carnival because the event was seen by unionists – and some nationalists – as a tricolour day, and a show of republican domination of public space in the city centre. At that time the Council flew the union jack every day of the year. For the next seven years Republicans had challenged the status quo and pushed for flying the Irish tricolour on the City Hall. Voting in late 2012 and the public consultation that followed led to a change. The flag would be flown on the eighteen days only.

This was a democratic decision taken under the proper procedures. However, the vote to restrict the flying of the flag precipitated an immediate mass protest from unionists and loyalist groupings and individuals, and saw a resurgence in death threats to politicians, attacks on political party premises, the blocking of major roads, violence towards police and counter-demonstrators, street rioting, personal injury and criminal damage leading to the closure of some businesses and widespread negative international media coverage – and a source of aggressive debate on the local airwaves.

Veronica looked for other and contradictory versions of events, comparing these accounts with her own notes. There was nothing at odds with the core of the story. Some sites named individuals and their proclamations that cultural and human rights were being abused. Others quoted politicians on the two sides of the debate, and the middle ground party that was the most virulently loathed by the flag protesters.

Veronica sighed as she read accounts of leading figures saying that of course they condemned violence on the streets but that people could not be pushed too far.

"So it's okay to set the place on fire if you feel you don't get one hundred percent of what you want?" She was talking to herself, as was normal procedure when chewing over the endless outraged claims and counter-claims. She yawned involuntarily, rubbed her eyes and looked to see what time it was. Half one in the morning and she had been pouring over these details for three hours.

She now seriously wondered why she had been so keen to convince Barry Doyle he should have Eliza on the show to discuss this running dispute. And how she could possibly have imagined they could make it enormously funny? Frustrated by the intractable nature of the fight about flags she still could not let go of the idea – somewhere at the back of her mind there was an angle. It was too late now to think any more about it, but she'd sleep on things and talk it over with Barry.

* * * * *

Chapter Two

Barry Doyle was in full flight when Veronica arrived in studio the next morning. He was in ebullient form, cheerfully greeting studio guests and those phoning in. His endless enthusiasm for broadcasting was infectious and the daily production team came to life when the green light came on each morning.

Veronica took the researcher Emily Foster aside, asking, "Have you had much interest in the flags dispute in the past couple of weeks?"

"No, the few calls we got were clearly orchestrated and Barry didn't want to let them anywhere near the air." She looked at Veronica questioningly, "Why do you ask?"

"I met an academic – bit of a spoofer. That's her thing so I have been researching it, thinking we might do something really funny. I know it sounds a mad idea and after spending hours on the internet I wonder if I'm losing it, but my instinct is that we could do something. Anyway have a look at my notes and the file on Eliza Taunter and let me know if you think there's an angle for Barry."

"Any rush on it?"

"No, sometime this week will do fine. I'll run it past Barry and the two of you can see what potential it has. I'll need to get my thoughts together in the meantime."

The two women turned to give their full attention to Barry Doyle, doyen of radio as he playfully contradicted a senior member of the civil service, "You don't expect me or the listeners to believe that now, do you?"

The grey-suited public official was clearly unused to anything less than deference, even from the media, and reddened with clear resentment. "Actually, Barry, I do expect to be believed. These are the facts of the report!"

"Ah yes, the report. Well, what have you to say to Mrs Tilson?" He spoke in a neutral tone as he greeted the incoming phone call, "Mrs Tilson, what have you to say about the facts of the report."

A hilarious pantomime ensued as the woman caller contradicted the civil servant on a number of counts, citing UNESCO statistics and a large number of recent research reports. Barry Doyle revelled in the controversy. Denying both of the speakers any further comment he closed the feature with "And there you have it listeners. You make up your own mind." In the background the sound of a seriously disgruntled civil servant could be heard tearing off his microphone and hissing a threat to report Doyle to the Controller. It added a farcical note to the whole business. A musical interlude provided the opportunity for him to talk to his team, addressing Veronica by name.

"Enjoying the pantomime?" He was at his happiest when challenging any part of the establishment. "Lunch at the Golden Palace anyone?"

Veronica was the only taker that day and she accompanied Barry to his favourite haunt and a decidedly lacklustre meal.

Over chicken nuggets, mayonnaise and iceberg lettuce she told Barry about the missing Nicola Tebaldi. "Have you come across him?"

"Nico, oh yes, a charming young man. Always beautifully dressed and what a body! Not my sort of course but a real young god." Under the apparent banter Barry was clearly concerned. "How long has he been missing?"

"I think about a week now but I'm checking out the details. He was supposed to house-sit for Jack Summers' father but didn't show up as arranged. Desmond's junior lad Sandy will know and I'm going over there after we've finished up here. I'll keep you in the loop – promise."

After another half hour the two had agreed on the main features for the rest of the week and Veronica had convinced Barry that if, and only if they could turn it into a really funny piece she'd bring Professor Eliza Taunter into studio.

"Sounds crazy but I thought it was all so ludicrous that you could turn it around. After some hours on-line my head was completely done in and I'm not so sure now. Somehow I can't let the idea go, but I'll not push it. Agreed?"

"Agreed oh great one!" He teased her mercilessly but only at times when they were in complete agreement.

* * * * *

In late September Botanic Gardens was already drenched in the red, yellow and orange of autumn foliage. The hot August hastened the seasonal changes in this northerly region. The Palm House flourished with rich tropical plants from more exotic climates, drawing a steady stream of visitors, and amongst them was Eliza's former husband, Leo Richards.

Richards had arrived in Belfast, unannounced and planned to finish his business as quickly as possible. He had no liking for Ireland or the Irish, and his brief experience there as a young soldier had not altered his fear of the place and his loathing for their politics. He wandered around mixing with a bus load of American tourists, admiring the lush, well-tended vegetation with little enthusiasm. He had half an hour to kill before meeting John Colliers.

Sir John Colliers was the esteemed President of the Royal Arts Society and a pillar of respectable Unionist society. Richards hoped that he could convince Colliers of the provenance of the pictures he was offering for sale, but relied on the fact that he was a man whose artistic choice and purchases were more venal than truly educated. Names meant more than nuanced aesthetics. Richards wandered behind two beautifully coiffed white haired ladies from the Southern States who talked incessantly. He looked at this watch. It was three forty five and his appointment was for four o'clock precisely. He had sufficient acquaintance with Colliers to know he should not be a minute late.

Although he had the pictures in his possession Richards planned to start negotiations with no more than digital images and a series of supporting documents which purported to show his legitimate ownership of the paintings. His proposition was that he was giving Colliers a first look and a chance to make a bid before the works went to auction in Dublin.

The inane and high pitched chattering grated, and the increasing humidity of the Palm House drove Richards out into the fresh air where he took a bench and sat patiently for the next ten minutes. Although he knew every brush stroke behind the digital representations he spent that time watching the computer images of paintings by Louis Lebrocquy, John Luke and William Conor. He would never have to work again if he could pull off this deal – or even half of it.

A Louis Lebrocquy painting entitled *Tinker Woman with Newspaper* from the 1940s set a world auction record for a living Irish artist, at Sotheby's Irish Sale in London in May 2000. The enormous price it fetched put Lebrocquy securely among a select group of British and Irish artists whose works had commanded prices in excess of £1 million during the painters' lifetime. Lebrocquy's painting technique used palette knife and strong, thick paint flows. He married in the late 1950s and set up his home and studio in the south of France, where his two sons were born. He died on 2012. The value of his work had therefore increased considerably since then.

William Conor and John Luke were two other artists whose paintings were much sought after. Richards had managed to acquire several of their putative works among his substantial portfolio.

* * * * *

Veronica was regretting having eaten those chicken nuggets as heartburn set in. She knew that Desmond had a virtual medicine cabinet in his salon as he frequently ministered unto his clients.

"So you lunched at the Golden Palace then?"

She nodded and gratefully accepted some brand medication.

"They will have to see about the catering – it's bordering on the dangerous!" Desmond's exaggerated tones were somehow soothing. "Anyway what are we going to do this afternoon? A hint of colour?"

"I am in your all-powerful hands Desmond – and happily so." Veronica sat back in the certain knowledge that her hairdresser would perform another of his near-miracles.

"Sandy will wash your hair and you can cross-examine him about Nico."

As the junior gently massaged her scalp Veronica felt no urgency about her inquiries and settled into a reverie under the strong soothing hands of the young assistant.

When he was applying the conditioner Sandy began, "So you've heard about Nico? It is very strange, I can tell you that. Nico is always reliable and he'd never let old George Summers down."

"Did he say he was going away?"

"No his parents are dead now so he only visits his grandparents, and that's occasionally even though he is close to them."

"And he wasn't planning a trip away somewhere else?"

"Not that I know of. We were supposed to meet last Thursday but he didn't show up. I've tried his phone but its dead."

Not wanting to sound as old and out of touch as she knew she was, Veronica didn't ask if Nicola had perhaps just forgotten to charge his phone.

"Have you got a number for him? I could ask somebody I know to trace whether it has been used recently."

Sandy produced a card, with Nicola's contact details. "It's the only one I have. Can you copy what you want?" He spoke with a strangled tone in his voice – although Nico was not gay Sandy had a huge crush on him.

"I'm sure we'll get to the bottom of this Sandy." Veronica managed to sound sufficiently convincing to reassure the lad. She had every intention of asking Jack Summers to do some detection work and track the use of Nicola's phone.

Passed back to the expertise of Desmond's skilful hands she abandoned herself for the next hour enjoying every moment of this self-indulgence.

As he was putting the finishing touches to her hair, Desmond asked, "Did Sandy have anything to say that was helpful?"

"Yes." She lied. "I have a phone number I can get a track on." She was not prepared to disappoint Desmond at that point. Veronica also had a strong feeling that she was going to solve this mystery, although there was nothing by way of evidence that she could follow up.

* * * * *

Wild Fern Alley had been getting a great deal of publicity, despite the abundance of hard stories in the press and broadcast media. Television cameras appeared at the opening and later at the ceremony where an award was made to the group for environmental and community improvement.

Then things turned very sour. Councillor Cobbles put out a news release critical of Wild Fern Alley alleging that some residents objected to changes being made without consultation. He was joined in his efforts by McVeigh and Stewart and another property owner by the name of Seamus O'Doherty – known to the group as Seamus O'Property.

Marianne was livid but refused to respond to media invitations for comment. Instead she put her efforts into contacting every resident to ascertain whether there were any complaints or objections. She understood this was a ploy to sow the seeds of distrust among the group and in the local community – but that was not going to succeed! As there were none she contacted other local Councillors to gain their support for Wild Fern Alley.

"I have emailed or spoken to all the residents – including students and there is no opposition or criticism."

"We are obviously in favour of this sort of project and the Green Party will support you." Rachel Johnston asserted confidently.

By the time the story went to print Cobbles had changed his version of events. He claimed that the residents had dug up the concrete surface of the Alley.

Marianne challenged him to his face. "And what do you mean by that? We took away some concrete to expose the original cobble stones – which are the preferred surface for run away in built up areas. Have you not read your own Council's policy on urban redevelopment – and don't you know your party's views on this?"

He shrugged and look blank. "I have a letter from the Department saying that repairs need to be done."

"Yes, repairs to restore the original alley! Johnno in number thirty one is an expert on the nineteenth century use of cobblestone you know! The concrete surface leaves it prone to flooding." Marianne was still sticking to the agreed group policy of keeping this a good news story – and avoiding any public confrontation.

A further account emerged when the local radio had interviewed local Councillors about the controversy. Brendan Cobbles quoted his partner in property, Shappie McVeigh. "These recycling bins could catch fire. They are a safety hazard beside this block of flats."

Marianne was shocked that the reporter did not question this ludicrous suggestion but remained silent – until the evening she came out to find Cobbles and McVeigh escorting Seamus O'Property along Wild Fern Alley – ignoring the protestations of an elderly woman. "How did you get in here?" She demanded an explanation. "You have no right to keys!"

They sneered at her and walked away leaving two gates unlocked and open.

Thaddeus came out hearing Marianne's raised voice and calmed the situation by coolly following the men and locking the security gates.

The next stage would be open hostility between Marianne and the landlords. However, she had yet to tell Veronica Pilchard about this antagonism.

* * * * *

The sun room at Marianne's was empty when Veronica emerged from her shower for coffee and the first cigarette of the day.

No other guests had stirred. It was six thirty and she had slept well if not for long. She took a few sips of the strong black coffee she had brewed and flipped open the phone. There were several messages but the most welcome and least expected was from Margaret, Lady Beightin. She lit a cigarette and opened the message.

"Had a wonderful cruise until the ship was struck with some mechanical problem, then a ferocious storm so we went into port in some Adriatic town, where the dreaded tummy bug hit the ship. At my age I can do without that so I decided to trek back overland. It will take some time so keep me posted about your own news. Yours aye, M."

Veronica felt a twinge of regret, realising how much she missed her friend and confidante. She also had to admit that she was missing Glenbannock after a fortnight in the city. She drew on her cigarette, exhaled and sighed, reluctant to tell Margaret how she felt just at that moment. She hastily replied. "Am in Belfast working and looking for a new place to live – will explain later. Otherwise fine and busy with Barry. VP" There was no need to mention that she had met up with Jack Summers again, or that Harry was being a pig.

By the time she had dealt with her other emails and messages Margaret had responded.

"Harry being a swine then? Have been thinking about our last case – is my intuition letting me know that you are about to embark on solving another mystery? S."

She tapped a quick answer "Yes to the first and probably not as regards the second. Let me know when you get home and I can tell you all." She hoped that Margaret would take a direct route home, only slightly ashamed at her selfishness.

* * * * *

Nicola Tebaldi woke to the sound of the front door slamming shut. He could hear some muffled talking in the distance but could not make out the words or whether it was one or more people speaking. Straining to hear he put his ear to the basement door. Thin dawn light came through the cobweb caked glass on the small window.

The voice disappeared as quickly as it had materialised. He might have been hallucinating or just imagined the voices. He was unshaven and badly in need of a shower. The bucket in the corner was stinking and he felt nauseous. This nightmare made no sense. Tears welled up in his eyes and he swore loudly in Italian to restore his sense of rebellious refusal to accept his incarceration.

The large box of French breakfast cereal was almost empty but he was so hungry that he devoured the last of its contents and what water was left in the one remaining plastic bottle. Nicola was not religious but had experienced an upbringing that habituated him to prayer in times of adversity – and this morning he got to his knees, crossed himself and prayed fervently for delivery.

He thought of his grandparents. Old habits die hard and Nicola, who had been raised as a chapel going Catholic, resorted to song. He cleared his tight throat and began to sing the Panis Angelicus.

* * * * *

Having finished with her messages Veronica went into Marianne's garden for some of the still fresh morning air, as yet almost unpolluted by petrol fumes. She was sitting quietly enjoying the peaceful start to her day when she thought she heard a voice faintly, singing and then weeping. It seemed to be coming from the house or garden next door.

"Hello? Are you in trouble?" She called out towards the adjacent garden.

Getting no reply she called out again as she made her way to the connecting fence.

"Hello?"

She heard a tapping noise, as if on a window but all the curtains were pulled in Eliza Taunter's house. The tapping continued and she moved her gaze down to the ground and realised there was someone gesturing wildly from behind a dirty basement window.

"Oh dear God!" Veronica was shocked and horrified. Without stopping to think of the consequences she stepped on the garden chair and leapt over the fence. She landed awkwardly, cursing and hoping she had not twisted her ankle as badly as if felt.

Shaken she got to her feet and went over to the well of the garden and the basement window. "Hello. Are you in trouble?"

"Dio Mio! Thank you!" The man spoke in a croaky voice with an Italian accent.

"Are you Nicola Tebaldi?"

"Yes. Can you help me get out please?"

"Yes, I will get someone. I'll ring immediately." At that she flipped open the phone and called Detective Inspector Summers.

At seven in the morning Jack Summers was just about to get into the shower when his phone rang. Reluctantly he decided to answer the call.

"Hello Jack. I've found Nicola Tebaldi!" Veronica was breathless with excitement and apprehension. "Can you help? He's locked into Eliza Taunter's basement!"

"What?" He sounded irritated as if he did not believe her. "What do you mean you have found him?"

"I was in the garden and thought I heard someone singing and weeping. When I went to look I saw him – the place is empty. Eliza is away at some conference but Nicola is in the basement. Can you get in there and let him out?"

Jack was cautious as it was not normal procedure to break into a person's house, but then it was not normal to have someone imprisoned in the basement. "It was sure to happen, with you about,

Veronica Pilchard!" He sounded both amused and determined to help the prisoner effect escape.

Jack arrived, unshaven and hastily dressed, within a few minutes, bearing his set of strictly unofficial keys – for use only in circumstances as dire as this. He had to take the same route as Veronica. His approach was steady and sure footed and he leapt over the fence with manly athleticism – in stark contrast to Veronica's clumsy arrival.

"Show me!" His voice was authoritative and she complied without a thought.

"Here!" Veronica was relieved to have an accomplice. "Can you open the back door?"

"Yes, I think so – but you look the other way! This is not official practice, as you well know!"

Jack Summers was not about to wait for a signed search warrant and deftly played the lock. "I'll take it from here Veronica."

"Fine, just get him out!" She was so relieved to have back-up that she was not going to argue.

A weeping and immensely grateful Nicola Tebaldi emerged in the morning light, blinking as he stumbled from the house.

"Let's get him into Marianne's." Jack felt relieved that Nicola was able to walk and was not apparently hurt. Addressing the young man he said, "You can explain once we get you settled and some hydration – you look as if you need it!"

"Thank you." Nicola followed meekly and in sort of stupor.

Having finished a small drink of water, a large coffee and croissant Nicola enjoyed the luxury of using a proper toilet. As he returned to the sun room the urge for a cigarette overwhelmed him.

"After all you have done to help me I am ashamed to ask, but could I have a cigarette, please?"

"Yes, of course!" Veronica thrust the packet and a lighter across the table. "I am sure you could use a smoke after all this time."

As he exhaled he began his story.

* * * * *

Nicola Tebaldi had been in Wild Fern Alley watering the large raised bed of herbs that George Summers added to the communal display, just as the light was fading. He noticed a man coming out of the back entrance to number seven Montague Road – home of the odious Professor Taunter – and struggling with a large bundle.

"Can I help you sir?" Nicola retained the courtesy that had been drummed into him as a young boy staying with his grandparents in a farm near Verona.

Richards did not recognise Nicola and grunted a reply, "Uh, no I have it."

"Ah, sir, you are the husband of Professor Taunter. We met at the McClintock Institute."

This recognition had transformed Richards' demeanour. He stood up and, smiling, put his hand out. "Yes, of course. Forgive me I am somewhat preoccupied."

Nicola approached and shook his hand. "Are you coming to live in Belfast?" His question was genuine.

"Ah, no. I am just on a flying visit. Eliza is in the Middle East for a month so I popped in to collect a couple of things." Richards looked at his watch. "Have you time for a drink? I apologise for being off-hand earlier."

"Thank you." Nicola had never been in the professor's home and was curious.

The last thing he remembered was sitting in an armchair sipping a glass of rather good red wine.

Nicola Tebaldi had known the man who had tricked him into drinking whatever concoction it was that had instantly drugged him, but he did not know the man's name. The police checked this immediately and got the information. They had no evidence as to whether Richards was still in Belfast as his known address was in Manchester and in days of peace in Northern Ireland air travellers no longer had to fill in details of the purpose of their visit and their destination for the security forces.

Leo Richards was at that moment waiting for his flight from Manchester to the South of France, unaware that his victim had been rescued.

* * * * *

Making out his official report DI Summers was careful to be as vague as possible, but acknowledged that Veronica Pilchard was neither a stranger to him nor to the police. The coincidence that Nicola Tebaldi had been house-sitting for his own father, and that he'd disappeared without trace for a week made the break-in defensible – but only on the understanding that there was a credible possibility that the victim might be injured, even seriously in danger.

Detective Chief Inspector Bill Adams was his superior, at Jack's station in Donaghdubh, and was not a fan of Veronica Pilchard. However, since the incident had happened in South Belfast Summers' report was not likely to come across his desk. Jack desperately hoped he could safely assume that Veronica had not yet stepped on the toes of police investigators in Belfast and that he could plausibly describe her as a known and trusted source of information to him and the police service in the past. That was why, when she'd contacted him on this occasion, he had acted immediately in response. He was ambivalent about his method of gaining entry to Professor Taunter's home, implying that this action was more a matter of accident and luck than the use of illegal skeleton keys.

Given that he had to explain his absence from his first shift he rang the desk sergeant and gave an elusive account of events at Montague Road, claiming that he had to show up at the local station and give them a full report on what he knew about the kidnap and the young male victim.

Jack Summers knew enough about the good professor to realise she would almost certainly make a formal complaint and that this would generate some upheaval and a lot of paperwork. He also knew that she would be grilled by local detectives about having a captive incarcerated in her basement. On balance, he reckoned, she would have the sense to take the easier option of dropping her complaint and hope that Nicola's statement exonerated her in this abduction. As kidnap is a most serious criminal offence, and could have resulted in Tebaldi's death, her pretentious remonstrations would only make matters worse. Jack's brief acquaintanceship with Eliza had not been pleasant.

* * * * *

Flying to Toulouse was, Richards imagined, the end of his time in Manchester. He would return to Belfast, in disguise and with another passport, to conclude his business, hand over the paintings and settle the sizeable financial agreement. Content in the knowledge that he would spend the rest of his days in a pretty villa on the French coast he savoured these last few moments in Old Blighty.

As his flight was called Leo stood up, glancing around suddenly alarmed to see his picture on the television. Horrified to read the subtitle 'wanted for kidnap' he walked hurriedly towards the boarding area. His stomach was knotted in fear and he was sweating because he was yet to dye his hair and botox his wrinkled face. Someone might well recognise him!

He would keep his sunglasses on until he had entered the jet and taken his allotted seat. There was no point in turning back as his plans had been carefully laid. As long as he could get out of Toulouse airport he was safe.

"Mummy I saw that man on the TV!" A small girl tugged at her mother's coat.

"Jenny, stop it. We have to get on the plane now!" The woman looked around but had missed Richards who had dodged into the men's toilet to avoid the possibility of any confrontation.

He dawdled behind most of the other passengers hoping that he could merge imperceptibly among them and prayed that he was not sitting near that brat.

For the entire journey he feigned sleep. On arrival he was one of the last passengers to disembark and walked slowly away from the luggage reclaim. Fortunately he had shipped what little he was taking to France and had only carried hand luggage on the trip.

The child was, mercifully, nowhere to be seen. Leo Richards left the airport, hailed a taxi and began his life as Peter Saunders, retired school teacher and British ex-pat.

* * * * *

Veronica Pilchard had initiated the dramatic release of the young Italian Nicola Tebaldi but in the process she had twisted her ankle badly. By the time she had made her full statement to the local police and left the station her ankle had swollen up and was growing more painful by the minute. Reluctantly she went to the nearest Accident and Emergency department hoping that in the middle of the morning she would not have to wait too long.

X-rayed, bandaged and advised to rest the injury she took a taxi back to Montague Road – feeling the need of strong coffee and a cigarette. On the short journey, which she would otherwise have cheerfully walked she rang the studio producer to say that she'd be available by phone but was going home to put an ice pack on her ankle.

Relieved to have escaped more serious damage, she got out of the taxi, paid the driver and hobbled up the path to Marianne's door.

The landlady was already acquainted with the details of the early morning rescue and greeted her with a smile and an invitation into the kitchen.

"Come in and tell me all. You can smoke and I'll get the coffee on – strong just as you like it!"

"Thanks Marianne. I feel a bit wobbly."

"Not surprisingly! Did you break anything?"

"No just a bad sprain. It should be fine if I keep my foot up for a day or so."

By the end of the day the all the residents knew about the dramatic rescue and Veronica Pilchard was co-opted onto the group – which she found very flattering.

* * * * *

Margaret Beightin returned to Glenbannock to find her gardener had mowed the lawns, dead-headed her prized roses and gathered the ripened fruit – some of which was carefully packaged under the shade of her front door. He'd left a note explaining that the soft fruits wouldn't keep but that he'd be sure to bring her some of his hen's eggs in exchange.

Molly Biggins had been in, done the cleaning and brought fresh milk and bread. She also left a note thanking Margaret for the postcards and promising to be back two days later. Molly was new to her employ but had sound references and had lived up to them in the few weeks before Margaret had embarked on her cruise.

This domestic tranquillity and a controlled sense of order was a welcome change from the noise and turbulence of her journey from the Adriatic coast. After two days of attempting to traverse Europe by train she had booked a flight for Belfast and home. She would not have admitted to anyone that she was well past the stage where travelling alone was a pleasure – and particularly with the addition of newly arrived migrants from North Africa in an already crowded Western Europe. She had never felt completely at ease with the numerous continental beggars that circled railway stations, and certainly not as they became increasingly aggressive during the 1990s. She was apprehensive nowadays as a lone woman with a slight but detectable limp and felt she was potentially a soft target for mugging. The world she had grown up in and travelled without a care had changed into a rather threatening place. Glenbannock was a haven of peace – a place where she knew everyone. It was good to be home.

Eager to catch up with Veronica she had emailed from the airport and was now reading the reply as she drank tea and looked out of the conservatory across the garden.

News that Veronica had sprained her ankle was not in itself disturbing but Margaret knew the injury was unlikely to be unrelated to some undercover exploit.

"Where are you and can I visit?" Margaret pressed the end button and considered the strong possibility that Veronica Pilchard was sleuthing once again.

* * * * *

The police in Belfast had extended the long arm of the law as far as Manchester in the hope of apprehending Leo Richards. By the time the Manchester constabulary had obtained a search warrant and forcibly entered Richards' apartment he had long gone. The place was furnished but nothing remained belonging to the man. His clothes, personal effects and documents were missing, although the rented flat was still in his name.

Even the rubbish bins had been emptied. In the basement the police searched the communal bins for possible leads but not a scrap of evidence was found. His bank account was closed. Leo Richards seemed to have disappeared into thin air.

At that point the decision was made to put this on national news.

When he had not been spotted within twenty four hours the story lost its edge and the investigation was put on ice.

* * * * *

The dramatic rescue of the kidnapped Nicola Tebaldi did not hit the news bulletins that day and Veronica made no attempt to publicise the event or her role in it. She did tell Barry Doyle what had happened but cautioned him to leave matters for the moment.

"Barry this is not a simple abduction. There is no apparent reason for kidnapping this young Italian. I mean he isn't rich and doesn't have wealthy family who could pay a ransom."

"And you think it is part of some bigger crime?"

"Yes. Why would this Richards man imprison Nico? In fact, why would he be in Eliza Taunter's house at all? They are divorced and she is out of the country." She grimaced in pain as she tried to shift her bandaged ankle. "Now I promise I will get you any exclusive interviews as and when there is some more information." She did not say that she intended to get that information herself.

"Fair enough. We have plenty for the show after today's hullaballoo!" Barry was still pink with delight after the morning's live debate and potentially libellous input of community activists and local politicians. "I hope this Taunter woman arrives back soon. This is starting to be a story with legs – and legs that will run for a fair distance!" Barry was in strident form but not with any self-importance or smugness. He simply enjoyed the rollercoaster of live broadcasting on the most controversial topics he could find.

I think she will be returning quickly, if only to inspect her possessions." Veronica cynically guessed that the draw of academic distinction and scholarly fame would be overshadowed by the lure of local celebrity on the subject of flags and the need to secure the contents of her home. Material matters and personal publicity enticed Eliza considerably more than the airless rooms of Middle Eastern conference venues.

"Can I assume that your temporary disability will prevent you from conducting a personal investigation, then?" Barry was only half-joking.

"That's a fair assumption." She lied, having already planned to get as much information from Jack Summers as possible and follow this up with beginning the process of gaining access to the scene of the crime – which could wait for a day or two.

* * * * *

Margaret Beightin arrived at number five Montague Road with a bouquet of flowers and a basket of fruit that evening. She was anxious to see for herself how her friend Veronica was keeping. Dressed in an elegant pair of tailored grey linen slacks and a light blue silk jacket she walked purposefully to the large entrance to Marianne's house.

"Ah, you must be Lady Margaret Beightin!" Marianne smiled and put out her hand to greet the visitor.

"Margaret will do. Can't bear formalities!" Margaret took the extended hand and was gratified that the response was a firm and warm grip. She judged people on their hand shake and degree of courtesy. "And you must be Marianne Kelly – of whom Veronica speaks highly! I am pleased to meet you." She spoke with warmth but less than sincerity – as Marianne's friendship with Veronica threatened to overshadow her own.

"Do come in. Veronica is in the sun room." Marianne gestured forwards to indicate the new guest might walk ahead and straight towards the glass walled room. "I will leave you two to chat." And with that the landlady seemed to evaporate.

"Margaret! How lovely to see you." Veronica almost got to her feet, but gave up as a surge of intense pain shot through her ankle.

"Don't get up, for Heaven's sake!" Margaret spoke commandingly – expecting to be obeyed. "I didn't come here to have you make your injuries worse!"

"Yes. Point taken. Anyway it is great to see you – it has been such a long time!"

"Less than four weeks – but I imagine you feel it is longer – what with all these dramas. Now tell me your news." She left the flowers and fruit on a nearby table.

The two women sat talking and exchanging news for the next hour. Veronica was reluctant to go into detail about the business of the house in Glenbannock but gave an outline of the details.

"Surely Harry was not always so truculent? I do agree about the smoking, however. Of course you won't want to hear that just now."

"No he seemed changed when he came home. I don't know why and he was not in any form to make conversation about that."

"So you are now looking for somewhere to buy?" Margaret asked in a voice that made Veronica suspect she had something in mind.

"Yes, but I want to stay here until I find somewhere suitable. I don't want to buy something just because I need a roof over my head and I don't even know where I want to buy."

"It's rather impractical to live in a bed room for more than a few weeks, Veronica – although I must say this is seems a pleasant enough establishment." Margaret had not lived in such accommodation for so long that she imagined the landlady locked the doors at ten at night and had a no-male visitors rule for lady residents.

Veronica took a deep breath, preparing to explain. "Margaret, I don't need much more room at the moment. When I cleared out my office I found I had a small box of things, and when I sorted out my wardrobe I only wanted enough to fill two suitcases. The rest is now in thrift shops. Harry wanted to buy the contents of the house – and especially his beloved kitchen so there's no a lot of moving to do." She'd not admit that she did feel rather like an itinerant student once again and missed her worldly possessions. It was embarrassing to own up to the fact that her identity was so bound up with the paraphernalia of everyday living – rather than some strong core of personal principles and individual beliefs.

"A fresh start then – and maybe no bad thing!" Margaret sounded rather like a friendly girl-guide mistress, providing Veronica Pilchard with a large degree of reassurance.

"Now tell me about your travels, Margaret." Veronica was eager to hear every detail of the Mediterranean cruise.

Margaret described the highlights of her travels, including the stopovers in Genoa, Naples, Sicily and Split. She had been very taken with Diocletian's Palace in Split and the modern museum in Syracuse. She omitted to recount her holiday romance with a retired army colonel which had been as torrid as it was brief. Margaret was not predatory in such liaisons but had a healthy appetite for firm if not young flesh, reminding her of her own athletic youth and many love affairs. Lady Beightin was certainly not the shrinking violet that DCI Bill Adams chose to imagine.

Margaret stayed for an hour, and then made her way to the opening of the annual Royal Arts Society exhibition, expecting to meet the wife of the President Sir John Colliers. She had enjoyed the company of Cressida Colliers during the cruise, as Margaret was a lone traveller and Cressida was there with her daughter Belinda.

Although Margaret and Cressida had been firm friends at school their paths diverged and now they only encountered each other occasionally. It was therefore a special pleasure for them to have time away from formal events and the chance to have conversations of some substance.

Cressida had braved the cruise for one day more than Margaret but as soon as Belinda fell victim to the norovirus they left immediately. Cressida was now unexpectedly home and had invited Margaret to the opening exhibition with enthusiasm.

"Do please come as my guest, Margaret. I was hoping to miss the round of arty chat, and false admiration." Cressida was not a willing first lady of the Royal Arts Society.

Margaret Beightin retained the sense of collegiate solidarity from her schools days and accepted the invitation with good grace – although in the hope that the exhibits would not all be the modern art school abstract works that totally baffled her.

* * * * *

Jack Summers had informed his father about the rescue of Nico and been instructed to act in loco parentis.

"Jack, the lad has no parents now. He has elderly grandparents in a farm near Verona. If he is willing and able to travel to them you must set that up for him. If he wants to stay in the house you make sure that he is properly looked after."

"Dad, I am not a total idiot. Nico has had a thorough medical examination and has spoken to the counsellor attached to the police. The only visible sign of trauma is that he has started smoking again." He made sure his tone was light-hearted and repeated his assurances that he would see that Nico was in good health, and might well take up the offer of a free trip to his grandparents. "Actually, what I have done is get him a new phone. I will get him to ring you when I hang up and you can talk to him yourself. Is that okay?"

"Grand, thanks Jack. I appreciate that. I was just worried..."

"That I'd been in the police so long I had forgotten both my manners and lost part of my humanity?" He guffawed.

"Now son, don't tease!"

Father and son ended the conversation with warmth. Neither wanted to concede the possibility that Jack had lost much of the tenderness he'd had as a young man. Neither was prepared to argue in what was apparently likely to be the last year of the old man's life.

"And I'll take care of the house Dad!" Jack sounded like the shy teenager he had once been. "I promise it will be clean and tidy when you get back."

It was the sad truth that Jack's father would not live much longer and had had chosen to spend his time in Italy rather than at home under specialist care and therapies that were unlikely to add a day to his allotted time. George Summers kept his own counsel on the subject however, leaving Jack with only a vague idea of his condition.

Not only had the middle aged policeman lost all hope of a marital reconciliation but he was about to lose his only remaining parent. The experience was changing his outlook and leading him into areas of thought he had never before considered.

* * * * *

The annual Royal Arts Society exhibition was as much a social as an aesthetic or artistic event. As President, Sir John Colliers was privy to all the decision of the selection panel, although in theory he did not influence their choice of exhibits.

The Royal Arts Society exhibition had a category of best new artist and more often than not the recipient was known to the President. Each year hopeful entrants made a point of crossing his path – and his palm. Colliers made a tidy sum in cash and in social cachet from this and his other honorary positions.

What he most coveted was national governorship of the BBC. Colliers knew plenty of establishment figures – being one of them – and made an extra effort to align himself with those who would appoint the incoming post-holder. He hoped that his wife would enjoy being party to that rather more than the Royal Arts Society.

For that reason he had welcomed the prospect of Lady Margaret Beightin attending the opening night. She was a woman of some importance, however much she despised the formalities of public office, and he was eager to be in her favour. If she endorsed a man it was an honest recommendation and thus her advocacy was seen as one hundred per cent legitimate.

Sir John and Lady Cressida were enthroned on the specially erected stage in the grand hall of the castle. Two other seats were reserved for invited dignitaries, of whom Margaret Beightin was one. As the artists, collectors, critics and earnest viewers mingled Margaret arrived, to find herself escorted to the stage, alongside the latest Secretary of State, Clive Heedon.

Margaret had met Colliers no more than a handful of times and found him personable if lacking in warmth and charm. She braced herself for the formal ceremony for the sake of her friend Cressida. Clive Heedon was a stranger to her and her first impressions were not entirely favourable. She shook hands with her hosts and the other special guest and took a seat – preparing for an experience rather like a poor sermon from a newly ordained minister. The event would be excruciating but must be endured and discussed in terms as kindly as possible. She was grateful that there was not to be a formal dinner to follow.

Heedon was a man of around fifty, sporting a thinning head of dyed blonde hair and an expensive sun tan. He was slightly stooped and his head nodded involuntarily when he got enthusiastic about a subject. His voice was reedy and nasal and he spoke in tones that deliberately attempted to obscure what was clearly a public school accent. He was probably the one person whose attendance the media would cover, and thus reflect on the glory of the President himself.

Clive Heedon was an avid if not educated art collector. He had found to his cost, having completely disregarded the advice of civil servants, that he'd been conned into buying fake works by local artists at a sizeable cost. Sir John Colliers had arranged that the dealer accepted a return of these pictures and thus saved him even greater loss of face – and though social media quickly spread news of these events the story never made the news.

Colliers had courted the approval of Heedon, and was pleased to have the Secretary of State in his debt, as his powers extended to influencing the appointment of the governor of BBC Northern Ireland. Tonight the President would introduce Clive Heedon as an aficionado of the arts and devoted collector of Irish works and invite him to open the exhibition.

Margaret found the abject toadyism nauseating and looked for an indication of how Cressida was taking this flattery. Her friend was standing bolt upright, straining to maintain a neutral smile but on further inspection she saw her folded hands had knuckles of ivory white. Lady Beightin nodded impartially and smiled towards her old friend with a twinkle in her eye. Cressida mouthed a silent 'thank you' in reply.

Both women were grateful that someone had scripted the Secretary of State a short speech, which was followed by a somewhat perfunctory announcement of the year's awards. In forty minutes the charade was over and they could drop the pretence, taking another and very welcome glass of wine.

"I must not overdo it Cressida. I'm driving."
"Bugger that! Margaret you were good enough to come to my rescue. You can leave the car at the castle and you will be driven home." Cressida looked at her nervously. "Unless that is you prefer to go before dinner?"

"In for a penny!" Margaret laughed. "Just tell me there will not be speeches!"

"Oh, no, John will spend the evening sucking up to Mr Heedon and his cronies. You and I can chat away – we don't have to network."

Margaret wondered how long Cressida had been so unhappy. Clearly these social occasions were anything but pleasant for her and she was merely there for show. And yet Cressida had made no mention of this during the cruise.

"And the food here is excellent – so it's a deal!" She winked conspiratorially at her old school pal.

The meal was potentially a trial for Lady Beightin, because she did not eat fish or any meat, and she was a moderate drinker. However, there was plenty of well cooked food that she could digest. In contrast Cressida ate heartily, at each course and consumed a large quantity of wine – without losing any composure. She relaxed as the next two hours elapsed and was genuinely smiling when they parted company.

Unlike her good friend Veronica Pilchard, Margaret Beightin was an astute judge of character and after the evening was over she held both Colliers and Heedon in fairly low esteem. They had shown the minimum of courtesy towards herself and Cressida, preferring to talk among themselves, huddled among a group of fawning cronies, laughing a little too loud and addressing the waiters in imperious tones. Cressida must have become inured to this boorishness. Either that or she covered her embarrassment and shame very well. Margaret was shocked that the wife of such a prominent man seemed to be so socially isolated – and had not kept contact with her friends from school or college. She resolved to keep in touch with Cressida.

* * * * *

Jack Summers had established that Nico preferred to remain in Belfast and did not want his frail grandparents to hear a word about his ordeal.

"The shock would kill Nonno!" He spoke in determined tones. "My grandfather has become very emotional with age and I am the only grandson he has. Promise me that they will not be told, please."

"Of course, Nico. Not a single word." Jack felt almost paternal towards the young man. "You need to eat up and put some weight on." He hesitated and then made a suggestion. "If Veronica is up for it do you fancy an Italian take away from Alberto's at her place this evening?"

"Oh yes! I'd love that!" Nicola Tebaldi beamed like a happy schoolboy. "I want to get her some flowers or something as a thank you."

"We can start with food – Veronica really enjoys her food."

Within an hour the three were seated in the otherwise abandoned sun room at five Montague Road, at a table groaning with the best of Alberto's fare and two bottles of good wine.

Marianne had tactfully rejected their invitation for her to join them. "I think you three have enough to talk about. Any other time and I'd gladly indulge."

* * * * *

Eliza Taunter returned to her home, having been informed of the kidnapping incident that had taken place on her property – in a manner that left her potentially under suspicion and therefore less likely to make a complaint about DI Summers.

The professor was at her most supercilious at the start of the formal interview but soon realised that the police were less easily impressed than her academic colleagues by her usual patronising tones.

"Professor Taunter I don't think you quite understand. This is a very serious criminal matter!" The uniformed sergeant particularly disliked the arrogance of academics, which he usually encountered through his duties concerning the university or – worse still to his mind – in the form of the graduate fast track new police officers. He therefore felt a raw gut dislike for this scrawny faced woman.

Eliza blanched and changed tack. "I apologise officer. It has all been very upsetting for me. I no longer feel safe in my own home." Her tone was less than convincing and she looked up at the uniformed policemen as he coughed.

"I think we should start at the beginning. Can you give me details of the dates when you were abroad and the contact details of anyone who has a key to your home, Professor Taunter, please?"

"No-one has access to my home unless I am there. And as I expected to be asked about my whereabouts I have written down the times, dates and travel details for the ten days before I was informed about this." Eliza Taunter was about to say incident but appreciated that would not sound sufficiently serious.

She left the police station having been warned that she was obliged to inform the police if she was leaving the country, but assuring the officer that she would not be going anywhere for the next month, other than to find a locksmith and have a full security inspection of her property. Chastened but also offended by what she felt was a lack of respect for her social and scholarly standing Eliza Taunter strode back towards Montague Road in a foul temper.

Seeing the BBC in the distance she decided she would accept the invitation to speak on the Barry Doyle show.

* * * * *

Margaret Beightin's taste in art was broad but did not extend to the post-Modern abstract. She had a decided preference for realism with a few exceptions, most notable amongst which was Louis Lebrocquy. She had a fascination for his portraits of famous heads, in thick multi-coloured oil paint applied against a white background. These pictures were realistic in that the people were recognisable but they held a spectre-like quality, seeming to exude a life force from behind the heavy tinted render – although they radiated a sinister sense of mortality. This engendered a sense of affinity with the pictures – rather than the artist or his subjects – and Margaret never missed the opportunity to spend time in the presence of this great art.

It was therefore with some interest that she overheard Sir John Colliers naming Lebrocquy in a telephone conversation.

"Oh, it's a real find!" Colliers whispered in a reverential tone. "A once in a lifetime opportunity."

Margaret was in the drawing room with Cressida Colliers having morning coffee. The room was furnished predictably with an old fashioned chesterfield suite, leather bound foot stools, a Persian carpet on parquet flooring and thick claret coloured velvet curtains drawn back with golden swags. The walls displayed well painted rural scenes encased in elaborate gold frames. She viewed the scene with reservation, deciding the choice was almost certainly Sir John's notion of taste, and ostentatiously expensive taste at that. Cressida would have chosen muted colours and watercolours – probably those of the late Tom Carr.

They chatted about their cruise and agreed that another such trip would require deeper research.

"I think that ship had seen better days!" Cressida stated. "And some of the passengers – well, really!"

"I agree about the ship. It wasn't up to much." Margaret pouted. "Of course there is always a chance that the dreaded bug will strike on a ship with plumbing like that." She laughed. Perhaps we are getting too fussy but I'd go for a smaller vessel and want tour guides with a rather better grasp of history."

Cressida chuckled, "Indeed, one would think that the guide would have known a bit more about Diocletian's Palace!"

"Anyway, perhaps next time we can arrange to go at the same time – or together if your daughter is busy."

"Oh, would you?" Cressida's voice exuded a pitiful gratitude.

"That's very touching Cressida. Not many people want to travel with me – I am rather too direct for most folk."

"Not at all, Margaret. I consider you a model of politeness." She sipped her coffee and added, "I thought you were very civil at the dinner and Mr Heedon is not the most gallant sort – is he?"

"I would never embarrass you Cressida. He is a toady and an obnoxious man but I was your guest and as such, I always keep such views to myself. I'd not be so reserved on a cruise ship – imagine being civil to a toad like that! One might give the impression of liking him and end up at the same table! Heavens no!"

"Then we are agreed. I would like you to be my travel partner next time." Cressida Colliers was delighted at this renewed pact of friendship.

"Actually, Cressida, I would be grateful for a travel partner. Coming back across Europe alone was rather a challenge – I'm past the stage where I enjoy solo trekking." This was both tactful and true.

Margaret rose to go and took hold of her battered leather handbag. She did not ask about Lebrocquy, mentally filing away that particular reference for later.

* * * * *

Chapter Three

It had been a week since Veronica Pilchard had discovered the ill-fated Nicola Tebaldi and Jack Summers had effected his release. Veronica's injury had healed remarkably, as she had complied with the advice given to her – which was quite out of character. She was now thinking that she should be searching for a more permanent place to live, and was indulging her penchant for expensive shoes and handbags so the room in Montague Road was fast filling up with her new possessions.

She missing having a proper home and admitted that a combination of broadcasting, her occasional mystery lover and Wild Fern Alley had become the centre of her life – to the exclusion of her close friendship with Margaret Beightin. As if on cue she got an email from Margaret that morning.

"Have you time to take in an art show today? It may be of interest. M"

Curious as to why Lady Beightin would think that she – as a notorious Philistine – should be in the least interested with art she confirmed her interest and asked for details.

The two met at entrance to the Stewart Gallery that morning. The gallery was a discrete but large display area stretching some hundred yards on the ground floor behind the furniture emporium run by Imelda Stewart. Imelda's husband Frederick ran the art business and counted many of the great and good among his most favoured clientele – including Secretary of State Clive Heedon.

Margaret had taken the precaution of bringing her calling cards with her, announcing herself as Lady Margaret Beightin, in the certain knowledge that this would impress Frederick Stewart.

"I'm dying to know why you think I'll be interested. I know nothing about art, Margaret."

"It may not be anything. Call it a hunch. I'll explain when we have been through the exhibition." Margaret smiled holding out one of her cards to Veronica.

"Ah! You are on to something!" Veronica's full attention was now aroused.

As they entered Margaret looked with concentration at the first large canvas she could see. It was a Basil Blackshaw and striking in its execution. The two women stood in silence until the owner arrived at their side.

"Frederick Stewart. A fine piece indeed."

"Yes, it is." Margaret offered her hand and he took it in a limp slightly moist grasp. She pushed down the immediate sense of revulsion – distrusting any man with such a handshake. "Margaret Beightin – Lady Margaret Beightin" she announced as she quickly withdrew her hand and pushed a calling card towards him. "My dear friend Cressida Colliers said you had a particularly good show on at the moment and I was determined not to miss it now that I am in town."

The card and the name dropping did precisely as Margaret had anticipated. Stewart was almost salivating. Cressida had bought a number of very costly paintings from him in the past and had impeccable taste in watercolours. Sir John Colliers was a man with whom he had done business over the years. What he lacked in aesthetic appreciation he made up for in his nose for profit and discretion – these two attributes being nearer to Frederick Stewart's heart than even the most exquisite of canvases. Art for him was much like any other property – except that it had a remarkable cachet and he liked prestige.

Veronica stood at her side, silently watching Margaret's expression – one of disgust thinly veiled by a rictus smile – and observing the obsequious Stewart as he fawned in the presence of a person who was titled and presumably wealthy.

Assuming an imperious manner she gestured towards the end of the gallery. "I think we should take in the whole exhibition now." She addressed Veronica, ignoring the gallery owner who took this as yet another indication of the woman's status and importance.

Veronica bit the inside of her cheek, the pain helping her to stifle the laughter rising in her throat. "Hm, indeed." She said no more as she was afraid her gleeful sense of mischief would become obvious.

Margaret walked slowly around the room that resembled more of an aeroplane hangar than a natural space for art. She rarely appreciated the huge canvases of contemporary painters. She stopped at a rustic scene of women stooped over buckets outside a farm cottage, painted in bold easy strokes of grey, blue and brown, with the tiniest of red and white flecks to enliven the scene. It was supposed to be a William Conor but Margaret knew it was too studied to be anything but a counterfeit – albeit a good one – and she knew there were many such pictures masquerading as the work of artists whose work commanded high prices. The tell-tale fingerprint irked her – it was just too crude. That was a faker's trick she'd seen before.

Margaret Beightin was aware of the rumours about local art dealers which is why she had chosen to visit the Stewart Gallery – a place where genuine pieces were on sale alongside those of a less secure provenance.

When she felt they had spent sufficient time looking at the exhibition Lady Beightin pulled herself up to her full height, drew back her shoulders and stated, "Mr Stewart these are rather good but I was hoping you might have something really special."

"Indeed? Lady Beightin I have a number of very particular works in my safe room, and I have contacts I can follow up if that helps. What did you have in mind?"

"Louis Lebrocquy. I am almost fanatical about his work but it so rarely comes on the market these days." She implied that she already possessed works by Lebrocquy.

"Really! I must say that Lebrocquy's work is very special."

His expression reminded Margaret of the cartoon characters sporting bulging eyes with pound signs in them. She had his total attention. She now spoke in a brusque manner, "And do you have any such work in your safe room?"

"I have to say that I do not. However, I have heard reports that at least one Lebrocquy is about to come on the market. Unfortunately, as I understand it, the painting is a relatively minor work."

"Oh, how marvellous!" Margaret switched tone, positively gushing at the obsequious dealer. "I am so pleased to hear that. Mr Stewart, you have my card and I expect to hear news as soon as the picture becomes available."

"Lady Beightin, I can promise you that you will be my priority client in this matter. Now I cannot guarantee the financial details."

He did not get time to finish his sentence as Margaret retorted, seemingly offended, "Mr Stewart, money is not an issue when it comes to great art!"

"Forgive me!" He cringed and bowed to her.

"Of course, just as long as I remain your priority." She decided against shaking his hand and gave a curt nod of the head. "I look forward to it." Turning to Veronica and assiduously avoiding calling her by name she said, "Now, my dear come along we have other business to complete this morning."

Without a word Veronica walked briskly behind Margaret into the bright morning sun.

Outside and some yards from the premises Veronica broke her prolonged silence. "Margaret what a performance! You were superb!" She grinned, "Now tell me. What is this all about?"

"I overheard a prominent person whispering Louis Lebrocquy's name on the phone and decided to act on my hunch that it is connected with some nefarious deed or other."

"That would your friend Cressida's husband?"

"Precisely. Lebrocquy's work was once among the most expensive of any living artist in the British Isles and although there are no known counterfeits, the value of the genuine articles still commands vast sums – and the gentleman in question is a deeply venal man who just happens to move in the upper echelons of the art world here."

"And when the painting comes up for sale you will be notified immediately! How cunning you are, Margaret."

"From you that is a great compliment Veronica." Margaret was particularly pleased with herself on this occasion.

Veronica left her thinking how unpleasant it would be to find oneself on the receiving end of Margaret's sharp tongue.

* * * * *

Marianne was determined to find out who the mystery man in Veronica Pilchard's life was. Veronica had obviously eyed up all the men in the residents' group and finding no takers in the romantic takers she had gone elsewhere. She knew he was dark haired and had a moustache. She knew that he was often on the surrounding streets, where they had met but that was all she could extract by way of specific information. As a landlady Marianne had a keen interest in the welfare and business of her guests. Veronica, however, was tight-lipped on this subject so Marianne would wait and watch in the hope of discovering his identity.

Coming from the rather narrow social circle of the tennis club for so many years, and now mixing in the fairly exclusive gay scene in the Golden Palace, Veronica found him almost exotic with his deep brown eyes and his silent way. What others might have seen as secretive and even devious she appeared to consider mysterious. As he was younger than her Veronica did not harbour illusions of a permanent liaison. She did however enjoy the excitement of the affair and the intensity of his attentions. Mitchell was not like the men she had known before. The sex was fantastic – which added considerably to his attraction.

She was not going to reveal his identity by telling Marianne or anyone else who asked – at least not yet!

* * * * *

DI Summers was informed of his father's death by telephone from the local police in the village nearest to the villa where George Summers stayed in Tuscany. Like most public servants in that region – nick-named Chianti-shire because of the vast numbers of British ex-pats who retired there or kept a summer home – the officer spoke perfect English.

Dottore Giacomo Dilucca was of course not a doctor but held the putative title as a senior Italian police officer. He addressed Jack with warmth as well as the professional courtesy he felt due to a fellow policeman.

Dilucca informed him that his father had passed away, peacefully in his sleep at the villa where he rented a tiny apartment. "It would have been a mercy Dottore Summers, as you know, since he was so ill."

Jack was taken aback. He knew his father was suffering from some incurable disease but George Summers had determinedly avoided the specific nature of his condition so that Jack did not know precisely what the ailment was. Of greater concern was the fact that his father had expressed his wish to be buried in Tuscany.

"Dottore Dilucca, my father wished to be buried in Tuscany. Is that not an extremely complicated and bureaucratic procedure? I am more than happy to comply with my father's wishes but I am not familiar with all the arrangements that must be made for someone who is not Italian to be buried where you are." Jack's voice resonated with a combination of shock and boyish innocence. His father had said that this might be his last stay in Italy but he had taken it more as a sign of age than anything like the fact of the matter.

"Please call me Giacomo and I shall call you Jack." Dilucca outranked the Irish policeman but felt this was a situation for geniality rather than any formality. "Things can be arranged through us at this end – if you can make your way here to sign the documentation and agree to the arrangements which are most ..." He hesitated, clearing his throat and searching for the right word. "The arrangements which are the least bureaucratic and time-consuming."

"Thank you Giacomo. Thank you very much. That is most helpful. I can fly to Pisa directly as soon as I have permission for leave."

The two exchanged personal numbers and agreed to stay in close touch.

* * * * *

Veronica sat in studio, as the Barry Doyle Show was about to start, beginning to wonder if her spiteful intent might not backfire. On the other hand Eliza had been determined to take up the invitation that had been emailed to her before she had returned early from the Middle East.

Although she had provided Eliza with a perfectly good face-saving pretext for postponing the live broadcast the professor had insisted that 'the Nicola incident' as she referred to the abduction, did not reflect on her at all. "Oh, that's all in the past. I wasn't even here and I would enjoy the opportunity to share my analysis with a – well let's say wider audience."

Now the academic was seated alongside Loyalist flag protester and community activist Dwayne Butcher, opposite Barry Doyle. They chatted for the few minutes before the show started.

Eliza began her well-practised speech, "*Flags are contentious and discourses around them are inconsistent. For example, flying the Irish Tricolour in St Patrick's Day parades and the Union flag in the Twelfth of July Orange parades are powerful symbolic messages of exclusion. These sustain bitter divisions and hostility between factions.*

Insofar as national flags express so-called 'identity' such displays are concerned with the sovereignty and constitutional status of Northern Ireland. And, the convenient equating of constitutional issues with 'culture' and 'identity' serves ethno-political purposes, for some political parties and all paramilitary groups. Different parties use plurivocity – that is multiple versions of meanings – and intertextuality – the shaping of meanings by use of other contexts – in their narratives on flags. Flags, emblems and symbolism visibly manifest division and hostility in everyday life in Belfast; with implications for politics and the entire peace process."

Barry laughed to himself. He was going to really enjoy this.

Dwayne Butcher looked at her in astonishment. "What are you talking about?" He was genuinely confused and unable to take in a word she said.

Eliza look down her nose at Dwayne, making a fundamental mistake as Mr Butcher was an astute and intelligent man, though evidently not highly educated.

"I think we can talk more about this when the show starts." Barry put his headphones on, as if taking production from the other side of the glass. He nodded at Veronica, indicating his intention to defer any further talk until the phone lines were open.

Barry let the bold professor talk about plurivocity, multiple versions of meanings and intertextuality for just long enough to see the switch board light up.

"Calls are coming in already folks. I think its Dwayne's turn to have his say." Barry Doyle gave instruction is a light neutral voice nodding to Dwayne Butcher.

"I don't know what intertextuality means. Is it something to do with gay rights?" Dwayne grinned mischievously watching for Eliza's response.

Her neck reddening and her jaw clenched tight she replied "Mr Butcher, you are playing the fool but I know you are a shrewd operator. Do you deny that protests about flags are just a pretext to raise your own public profile?" She stared straight at him, thinking herself winning the argument.

"No, this is about our culture – about our right to have the national flag flown every day of the year." Dwayne Butcher had prepared himself for the interview.

Barry Doyle cut in. "I think the listeners have something to say. Let's take line one and Billy."

"The union flag is British and Belfast is British – can the professor's fancy words change that?"

Settling in her seat, lowering her shoulders and breathing out Eliza Taunter began, "Billy, I wonder if you know about the democratic system where votes decided the matter." Her tone was unfortunately so condescending that Billy retorted.

"I wonder if you can speak the Queen's English!" And he hung up.

Dwayne broke in, "The question is not about democracy. It is about the denial of our rights. Look to England where the flag flies every day in municipal buildings in London, Liverpool, Manchester, and other cities. I know 'cos I checked the facts."

"We'll take another call. It's Mary on line two. What do you think Mary?"

"Flags have always been controversial here. As far back as the late 1940s and again in 1953 with the Queen's coronation, when nationalist Councils like Newry refused to fly British flags and emblems." The caller paused to give her words added weight. "The Unionist government passed laws to see that didn't happen again, but now we have rules about when flags are flown on government buildings. This settled things."

Anxious not to be outdone and eager to display her extensive knowledge on the subject Eliza replied. "Unfortunately those rules do not apply to local government buildings, Mary." Again her tone was patronising.

"Look you professor. Flags and emblems are a matter or respect and equality. By the tone of your voice you don't do either of those! That's all I have to say." The line went dead.

"We certainly are touching on raw nerves this morning." Barry cackled. "Let's take another caller."

Some half hour later the calls were postponed for the news. Dwayne was relaxed and content to repeat what he had stated from the beginning. Eliza was tense, unsure of how many more insults she could absorb from the unwashed and uneducated who were calling in.

During the news break Barry ascertained that the remaining calls were for the professor, and they were increasingly anti-English and mostly sexist.

Veronica considered the professor to be the maker of her own misfortune but felt she should not be subjected to the incoming tirade. She spoke from behind the glass, "Barry should we go to the package after the news?"

This was a cryptic message indicating that remaining calls would be gratuitously insulting.

"Remind me again, Ms Pilchard." He addressed her in this way that signalled agreement.

Barry Doyle was a consummate broadcaster and tactful show host. Lying, he said there was a technical fault with the phones and thanked them both. "Pity to cut things short." He gestured towards the door as his research assistant came in.

"Can you show our contributors out, Emily? Thank you for coming in – much appreciated." He got them off air in a flawless display of professionalism, knowing Veronica was right to draw this farce to a close.

Barry considered reading some of the text messages that came up on his screen. Professor Eliza Taunter had stirred up a hornet's nest of hostility and xenophobia. Instead he announced to his listeners that the incoming messages he could see were personal and a few obscene. "Even Barry Doyle has standards!" He chortled and pressed the start button on a prepared package on fracking in Fermanagh. That was contentious enough to set the phone lines ringing before the feature was half way through.

While he worked with the many and varied callers to his programme Barry knew that the collective memory had a very short span and feelings about fracking would create an immediate distraction.

* * * * *

Jack Summers took the flight from Belfast to Pisa, armed with hand luggage, basic Italian and a fist full of Euro to smooth his way in case credit cards failed to be adequate. He was in still shock from the news of his father's sudden death but the information had registered sufficiently to cause him that aching sense of loss he had experienced as a boy when his mother died. The pain of that bereavement had stayed with Jack throughout his teens and adult life, somehow gnawing silently away the core of his emotional development and his capacity to form lasting personal relationships.

Giacomo Dilucca was at the airport to meet him – in civilian clothes and a large card on which Jack's name was printed in capital letters. The sight of the tall handsome man in jeans and a sweatshirt was profoundly reassuring. He'd expected Giacomo to be there but the physical presence of someone who had both local knowledge and authority made the prospect of his time in Tuscany much less daunting.

"Jack!" Giacomo Dilucca stood at the entry to the luggage reclaim with his hand extended.

"Giacomo. Thank you very much. I appreciate that this is a long way from your patch and long after your day should be over."

"Not at all, my good friend." Dilucca grinned. "I pulled rank and got a driver for us. Is that all your luggage or do you need to go to the reclaim?"

"No that's all I brought." Jack held up an old leather overnight bag that looked as if it had seen a fair few years' service.

"Then let's be on our way."

The two men strode out of the air conditioned arrivals section into the remains of the strong heat of the day, dropping their pace in the few hundred yards it took to reach the police car.

"After you!" Giacomo opened the back door and ushered Jack in as the driver took his bag and deposited it in the boot.

"Have you eaten?" Dilucca said in a voice he could have used with a close friend.

"No, I am not a great fan of airline food and I was not hungry."

"Perhaps when you have had time to settle and have a drink." Dilucca sat back and watched the urban scenery pass by until they reached the tree-lined country roads taking them over and across the Tuscan hills.

Jack looked through the darkened glass of the police car feeling numb, tired and grateful for this brief period of respite, deciding that he'd postpone thinking about food and hotels until they got to their destination.

After twenty minutes or so Dilucca said expansively, "This is fine country Jack. I know your father loved living here. I didn't mention it before but I have met your father, and he was a good friend of my father-in-law."

Jack turned to him, staring into Dilucca's face. "You knew my father?"

"Yes he was a frequent visitor to our home. Perhaps you would give us the pleasure of staying with us for this difficult time?" The invitation was gracious, making it difficult for Jack to refuse.

"That is more than generous Giacomo. If it is not an imposition I would appreciate that, at least for this evening. I am all over the place."

"Then it is settled!" The policeman flipped open his phone and pressed a pre-dial number. "Lucia? My good friend Jack will be with us for his stay. We will be home in half an hour." He tapped the glass partition that separated them from the driver. "Mario un po piu rapido, per favore." At that moment the car sped off breaking the speed limit, raising a powdery wake along the narrow dusty road.

They arrived at a hill top villa, surrounded by pine trees and bougainvillea at the end of a long wide driveway. At the front door a woman and an old man stood to welcome them. Lucia and her father waved as the car came to a halt.

Lucia Dilucca's father was a man of around eighty who spoke English with a thick Tuscan accent. He had known George Summers for forty years and embraced Jack warmly when he got to the front door.

"A very fine man. Your father was a good friend and I am sorry for your loss." The old man spoke with tears in his eyes.

"Welcome Jack Summers." Lucia extended her hand. "Our home is your home at this sorrowful time."

A young woman servant appeared, curtseyed and took Jack's bag.

"This is Cici our life-saver!" Dilucca said in a cheerful tone. "She will show you your room and call you when the food is ready." He bowed his head in a tiny movement and nodded.

Jack walked up the wide staircase and along the corridor to his allotted room. Dilucca and his wife were polite and warm in a way that allowed him the space to recover his composure after the old man's emotional greeting – which had brought him to the verge of unmanly tears.

He took a shower, changed his shirt and sat by the open window for the intervening minutes before he was called for dinner. Outside birds sang from the perfumed darkness. He was a world away from the drab urban setting of College Road in Belfast. The luxury of the villa, the gentle Italian autumnal environment and this unexpected hospitality did not soften the shock of his father's sudden death, but it assuaged his worries about making the funeral arrangements.

Dinner was an informal buffet set out on a long wooden table in a veranda that stretched forty metres along the back of the house. Bowls set out along the table offered breads, cold meats, roasted vegetables and salads. Decanters of local wine and iced water were set out by Cici as they sat down.

"Please help yourself Jack." Lucia gestured along the table. "You may not be hungry but I imagine you have not eaten since you first spoke to Giacomo."

"Lucia's father has gone to bed and sends his apologies. He in nearly ninety and sleeps early these days."

"I am surprised to hear you say that. He looks much younger and a fit man." Jack's enthusiasm showed his sincerity.

"I will tell him tomorrow – he will be flattered!" Lucia said with a smile and a nod.

Giacomo Dilucca had decided that he did not need to make the usual explanations which he extended to new guests at his home, but felt it might be a useful topic of conversation as an alternative to discussing the recent death.

"Now, Jack, I must explain that this magnificent villa has not come from the proceeds of police corruption – my salary is modest. Villa Valeria belongs to my wife, and was the property of her late mother. I am of much more humble stock."

"Giacomo! It would never occur to me!" Jack felt sure that his host was an honest man, although he sensed Giacomo was not telling him everything in connection with his father. "I hope I did not give you such an impression."

"No, not at all but I'm Italian and we are very nosy people. In this part of the world everyone wants to know where money comes from and to be truthful not all of my colleagues live on their salaries alone." He winked and grinned widely.

For such an apparently open man Giacomo was nonetheless inscrutable. There was much more to him than his genuine courtesy.

"I have to say your home is very impressive!" He did not add that he envied Dilucca this extravagant villa because he did not. "I assume that Lucia is from this area but are you also?"

"No I am from the Veneto, from a village near Verona."

"Isn't that a coincidence" Jack was suddenly attentive rather than making small talk. "My father has to have someone as a house sitter when he is in Italy – for insurance reasons – and the young man is also from a village near Verona. Nicola Tebaldi has been doing this for the last few years."

"A coincidence? I know his grandparents. Their farm is on the edge of Poggiduomo where I grew up!" Giacomo laughed out loud.

It was Jack's turn to keep silent on information – as he had promised Nico he would make sure that news of his abduction could not get to his grandparents. He shrugged.

Unwilling to be left in the dark, seeing his guest avoid the subject, Giacomo set politeness aside and took on his policeman's demeanour.

"So, what is that you feel obliged to hide? Has Nico got into trouble?"

"Oh, no!" Jack would ask his host for complete confidentiality. "He had an unfortunate experience and my father swore me to secrecy as the information would seriously upset his grandparents."

"If that was what your father advised it must be done."

"As long as you keep it confidential I can tell you – it's still really a mystery as to why, but the former husband of a professor at the university in Belfast tricked Nico into taking a drugged drink and imprisoned him in the basement of her house. I live nearby and a lady I know discovered him – we rescued him."

"When you say it's a mystery what precisely do you mean?"

"We cannot find a credible motive for abducting Nico. The professor was out of the country at the time and had been divorced from Leo Richards for years, so why was he even in Belfast? And what reason could he have for incarcerating Nico?"

"Perhaps he was up to something. Nico was a witness to his presence and therefore a threat. I take it that you have not captured this Richards man?"

As the two men talked, engrossed in police business, Lucia stood up and excused herself.

Jack was embarrassed. "Lucia, please forgive me. It is rude of me to talk of police work in your home and at your dinner table."

"Not at all. You have come to life again! I am glad to see that. I actually have some things I would like to finish off – it suits me to leave you two detectives to talk." Whether or not she meant what she said Lucia made them feel they had permission to continue the conversation.

The facts were simple Leo Richards had escaped the net of the English and Northern Irish police. His former wife had no idea that he had been in Belfast, how he had got into her home or what reason he had for his visit. Indeed she had been surprised that he had been inside her home as he did not have keys and had never previously visited.

Giacomo laughed as Jack described the convoluted negotiations that they hoped would lead Professor Taunter to drop her complaint about his forced entry to her home.

"She sounds like a woman with something to hide – in my opinion."

"Like many of the scholars who roosted comfortably at the university during troubled times she is a person of whom one can say that there is less to her than meets the eye. From rumour and gossip it appears she is rather an academic impostor."

"I'm afraid that is the case throughout the world my dear Jack."

As host Giacomo suggested a night cap and the two sipped vintage brandy in large glass globes before retiring to bed.

* * * * *

Belfast's university area lay under a cold dank mist rising from the River Lagan. Veronica Pilchard had slept badly, in part due to the distant but still audible night-time carousing of students and in part because she had a deep sense of apprehension – not that she could identify any reason for such foreboding.

It was not yet quite dawn when she went downstairs, made a pot of strong coffee and retired to the sun room for a cigarette. She sat scrolling through her lap top reviewing the features she had produced for the Barry Doyle show in the coming days. They were certainly dramatic enough to attract a huge audience response – which was essential if they were to meet the punitive targets set by Head of Programmes. Willie Jackson hated Veronica and was hoping they programme figures would not prove to be as massive as the first five sets of statistics demonstrated.

Veronica returned this antipathy and since she was not beholden to Jackson she took every opportunity to needle him. She enjoyed the fact that if the Barry Doyle show was a success it reflected well on her and that Jackson's pride was considerably greater than his ambition – to such a degree that he'd prefer lacklustre figures for London than admit Veronica Pilchard had outdone him. Age had not mellowed the doyenne of radio production.

Buoyed by these thoughts she temporarily put aside her computer and looked into the murky sky. All nearby houses were in darkness except for next door – where it seemed Eliza Taunter had slept equally badly. Veronica's instinctive predisposition for snooping made her acutely observant. Although she was a poor judge of character she was sharp-eyed in matters of the material world. She noticed a figure moving behind the net curtains in the one illuminated room. It was too large to be Eliza, and looked like a man.

Had it been anyone but Eliza, Veronica would have assumed the man to be a visitor or a lover – even if only for the night. However, the professor was renowned as a celibate and lacked all traces of common hospitality. The man must be an intruder.

Could she ring Jack Summers? He was only home from his father's funeral. He would probably dismiss her idiotic theory in any case. Veronica Pilchard put temptation aside this time. She returned to her computer and finished the few script edits required.

Just as she stood up to return to her own room she saw the stranger – as she thought of the man in Eliza's house – leaving from Eliza's front door, heaving a large package wrapped in dark cloth, and gently pulling it behind him. The light was still on in an upstairs room.

Veronica worked on for another hour and then set about preparing herself for the outside world, spending another hour washing and fixing her hair and applying make-up in as subtle a manner as possible – but carefully creating the look of a younger woman. She returned to the sun room for more coffee and her last smoke of the morning. At precisely nine she left her temporary home in Montague Road, walking briskly towards the city centre.

*****

At that moment Sandy Hughes was waiting with some trepidation in the corridor outside the Dean's office in the main Lanyon Building of Queen's University. This was the day of his disciplinary hearing, the result of which would determine whether he was permitted to continue his degree course.

He had prepared detailed notes so that he could make a logical and dispassionate case in his own defence. As he stood, in the mullioned hallway he reviewed this material.

"She failed me on both my assignments. She told me I should stick to trichology – that's hairdressing – and I admit I did tell her she was the queen of trick-ology so she reported me. However, I believe this was all because I disagreed with her in tutorial and questioned her theoretical proposition – which I understand is permissible in academia."

At nine twenty he was still waiting and beginning to feel somewhat aggrieved. He had arrived on time for a meeting at nine o'clock. The least the disciplinary panel could do was to offer some explanation for the delay but no-one had appeared. He could not walk away as this was his only chance to exonerate himself from what he believed to be a charge that was as spiteful as it was spurious.

He checked his phone but there were no messages.

When the Dean's deputy opened the door Sandy stood to attention.

"I'm afraid Professor Taunter has not arrived for our meeting, and she is not answering her phone." Assistant Dean Reynolds' demeanour was apologetic.

Deciding that ultra-politeness would do no harm Sandy asked, "How do we proceed now, Sir?"

"We can interview you Mr Hughes." Reynolds was returning the formal courtesy. "You are entitled to hear the precise allegations made about you and to make your case." He coughed and continued. "I see you are alone. You are permitted to have at least one student representative with you."

"I felt that I should simply report the facts from my point of view, sir."

Ushered into the plush surroundings of the nineteenth century office replete with heavy wooden book cases and a desk that looked as if it had been here since Queen's had first been furnished, Sandy felt the weight of tradition fall on him.

He took the allotted seat and waited for the Dean to start the formalities, rather relieved that the odious Eliza was absent.

Over the next fifteen minutes the Dean, his assistant and Sandy Hughes went over the allegations made by Eliza Taunter and Sandy was given the floor to make his case.

The Dean sighed as Sandy finished presenting the brief contents of his defence.

"Mr Hughes, I am obliged to take complaints by senior staff very seriously. However, in light of the fact that Professor Taunter has not seen fit to grace us with her presence, or to make a proper – or indeed any – apology I feel that we should err on the side of caution. I am minded to dismiss these allegations and to accept your version of events – and to do so on the basis that your record of academic achievement and your behaviour have been exemplary until this – ah - accusation."

He stood up and offered his hand, "Mr Hughes I am dismissing this complaint and any reference to this shall be expunged from the record."

Sandy shook his hand with a firm grasp. "Thank you sir. Thank you very much indeed! I am extremely grateful." He cleared his throat, adding, "And mightily relieved, to be candid."

Sandy Hughes nodded to Reynolds and was leaving the room when he heard the Dean saying to Reynolds – in a voice that was clearly meant to be audible, "That bloody Taunter woman!"

Sandy skipped boyishly down the corridor and ran at full speed across the quad. He was ecstatic – he'd been acquitted without a stain on his record! The heavy cloud had been lifted after the entire summer.

* * * * *

Jack was sitting reading the letter from his father, tears streaming down his face – his thoughts far from the vicissitudes of keeping the peace.

The letter had come through the circuitous route that is the Italian postal service, some ten days after it had been written, and he suspected its contents as soon as it arrived.

Giacomo had not been explicit but had hinted that George Summers was ready to meet his maker and from this Jack felt sure that his father had enlisted some help.

He could not bear to re-read the compassionate and paternal words again, now that he had got the facts.

George Summers had a serious complaint but it was not cancer. His specialist had identified the condition Alzheimer's disease just before the preceding Christmas. Over the spring the disease had taken its course more rapidly than the prognosis had estimated, so George put his affairs in order before leaving for his last stay in Italy.

Jack had sobbed aloud when he read the last words his father had written to him. "I didn't want to compromise you Jack. Not only because of your job but because it is an enormous burden that no parent should put on their child – both moral and legal. I hope you will forgive me. I have always loved you much more than my gruff exterior may have shown."

George Summers had known Antonio Breganza would help him get the pharmaceutical answer to his problems and that Giacomo and Lucia would take care of Jack when the time came for his funeral. He had said that by the time Jack got the letter he would have met Giacomo and Lucia and that they would have smoothed his path in making the necessary arrangements – as in deed they had. Lucia's father had taken on the task of procuring the most effective concoction of drugs without any explicit mention to his son-in-law, but with the tacit agreement of Giacomo, Lucia and of course, George himself.

The old men had gone to a local trattoria, at one time a hunting lodge, and fed on wild boar, pasta and duck that final evening. Antonio sat with George in his private apartment in the villa where he was ending his last stay. They drank grappa and toasted each other.

Without tears or obvious emotion George drank his preparation and they embraced warmly before George Summers lay down on his bed. Antonio sat for the few minutes it took his good friend to fall into his eternal sleep. He rose and left the villa telling the housekeeper he would return at six in the morning – informing her that his friend had given strict instructions not to be disturbed before that time.

It was Antonio Breganza who found the body of George Summers, looking peaceful. He wept bitterly and said a prayer for his departed friend of nearly half a century. Having washed his face in the adjoining bathroom he composed himself to make the call that Giacomo knew to expect.

Certificates were signed, payments and duties paid, with all the alacrity that came with Giacomo's professional status and the high social standing in which Antonio Breganza was held. Jack Summers would arrive at Pisa airport the following evening.

Now in the cold light of day, with a chilly mist rising from the River Lagan Jack thought of his father – whose ashes lay buried under a tree in the warmth of the Tuscan hills – and was glad that he had chosen to die in Italy. He felt utterly bereft with a loneliness that was physically painful. He hugged his stomach and groaned.

* * * * *

Not far from the City Hall Veronica was seated, shrouded in a hairdresser's blouson in front of a large bevelled mirror, looking glum.

"Now Veronica, don't fret. All you need is a trim and a tinge of colour and you'll be fine." Desmond soothed. "You didn't expect the last cut to survive for months, did you?"

"No, it's just that it has suddenly been a bad hair day every day!" She still had a premonition of some ominous event – and still had not rational way of explaining this foreboding.

As Sandy came in beaming he shouted "I'm off the hook! The old witch didn't even show up!"

"Tell all!" Desmond squealed in delight.

Sandy described Eliza's absence, his presentation of the facts and his exoneration in as much detail as he could manage to fit into his dramatic narration of the morning's short-lived events. "And as I left the Dean's office I clearly heard him say *that bloody Taunter woman!*"

"If the dear professor didn't show up to the disciplinary there must be something badly wrong – she's a spiteful cow!" Desmond declared with force.

Veronica frowned, "She was at home last night. I saw her light on just before dawn – and a strange man leaving her house a short time later. Why would she miss the meeting?"

"Well Sandy is in the clear – his reputation unblemished! I am happy to settle for that – who cares why that ghastly woman failed to show?"

* * * * *

Margaret Beightin did not have to wait long for news of the availability of a Lebrocquy painting. Frederick Stewart texted her a grovelling message.

My dear Lady Beightin you will be pleased to know that I will be in possession of a Lebrocquy within the next twenty four hours. As the priority client I wanted to inform you immediately and offer you a viewing at your convenience.

Margaret snorted, laughing out loud "Do I seem the sort of person who wants to meet in a toilet?"

The text continued. *In addition I am assured that there are also works by John Luke and William Conor and I will reserve you a first viewing of these also, if that is your wish. Sincerely Frederick Stewart.*

Knowing that a Lebrocquy painting was worth considerably more than a Luke or a Conor she considered whether it was worth pursuing the works of other great artists. However, she decided that showing a muted interest might be prudent. There might be no connection but it seemed rather a coincidence that these art works all surfaced at the same gallery simultaneously.

Before making plans for the viewing Margaret wanted to talk to Veronica, about this and the matter of her friend's living arrangements. While she understood that the temporary room was a stop gap, Margaret felt it was a precarious and quite unsuitable lifestyle – and Veronica was a person who needed security at this juncture. And, she did miss the regular visits and collusion with her pal in unearthing criminal complicity – in their exclusive friendship. Anyway Margaret wanted help with the mystery of the paintings – as she saw it.

Lady Margaret Beightin was regarded by her wealthy extended family as poor, lacking her own family and in need of their kind support. Her late cousin had left Margaret her cottage just outside Glenbannock. She was somewhat offended at manner in which this bequeath was made and the solicitor's condescension at the reading of the will. Swallowing her pride, only because she detested these relatives and wished to avoid a vulgar contretemps, she had nodded and thanked the assembled group, before hurrying off silently cursing their misguided efforts. In retrospect, some weeks later, she felt she could make use of the property by renting it to Veronica for a small amount until her friend decided on a permanent and more appropriate residence.

Since she felt Veronica might be offended by an offer of charity Lady Beightin was careful in presenting her proposition in an email.

"Veronica I have taken possession of a cottage – left to me by a cousin – and need time to decide what I shall do with the property. It is just outside the village. As I do not want the place lying empty would you consider taking it temporarily on for a modest rent? Since I am asking a favour of you I am sending my proposal by email so that you can turn it down by return if the idea does not appeal to you. However, if you are interested I am picking up the keys this afternoon and can let you have a look when you have time. Meantime the mystery of the paintings is unfolding – will tell you all when we next meet. Yours Aye Margaret."

She pressed the send button hoping that her friend would take up the offer and abandon her temporary and utterly unsuitable lodgings.

* * * * *

Sir John Colliers had taken possession of the five paintings early that morning. Posing as his agent, a cosmetically altered Leo Richards arrived at the Collier home by taxi and presented himself as Peter Saunders. Colliers did not recognise Richards now that his face was smoothed by botox, his hair dyed, eye colour changed with contact lenses, and his height increased by built up shoes. Although the voice was the same, the contrivance of a thick Scots accent disguised that fact.

At a deliberately early hour, just as dawn was breaking, Colliers escorted Richards into his study. "Mr Saunders, you are a welcome guest!" He was flushed with pride and exhilarated at the prospect of getting a buyer for the Lebrocquy immediately. He calculated that even with the commission for Stewart he would almost double his money.

Richards set the heavy cloth wrapped package on Colliers' desk. He calculated that he would make a small fortune from selling the Lebrocquy, and profit from the fake Luke and Conor paintings.

Colliers removed the packaging from the bundle, revealing five paintings, each separately bubble wrapped. He clipped the wrapping carefully so he could inspect each one in detail – for which purpose he had a large magnifying glass. Satisfied that he was examining genuine art works he smiled, turning to the man he believed to be Peter Saunders. "Fine! Now I believe that the deposit has been cashed, and the remainder will be in Mr Richards' hands within a day."

"He will be pleased to hear that Sir John." Richards was excessively polite, playing to Colliers' egotism. "Is there anything else that you require?"

"No I have the documentation – which has been scrutinised to my satisfaction."

Richards nodded and slightly bowed his head to acknowledge his host's superiority.

"Then I think the transaction is complete!" Colliers was eager to see the back of his guest and stood up. "Is your taxi waiting?"

"Yes, Sir John. I am on my way to the airport."

Colliers offered his hand and Richards feigned a limp grasp in response.

"Well goodbye, and give my regards to Leo!" Sir John Colliers was a very happy man at that moment. He watched Richards' taxi pull away from his home as dawn broke.

* * * * *

Veronica had left *Curl up and Dye* quite delighted with Desmond's handiwork but still preoccupied by what might have happened to Eliza Taunter. Her failure to turn up at the disciplinary hearing was very out of character. However, she was due to meet up with Barry Doyle and did not have time to follow her intuition.

Barry was in the Golden Palace, chatting with Bertie Norton when she arrived.

"Veronica! You have been at Desmond's and look fabulous." Bertie squealed with affectation.

"Thanks Bertie. It's worth every penny just for your flattery!" She smiled fondly at the young man who had become her friend by accident more than design. Veronica was grateful for the genuine affection many of the gay set in the Golden Palace showed her.

"So Sandy got off those trumped up charges against him!" Bertie had seen the tweet and all the details of the student's encounter with the Dean that morning – except for mention of the Dean's comment on Professor Taunter. Sandy was judiciously on social media on matters that might come back to bite him.

"Yes, indeed. I know she was at home last night – her light was on – so I can't imagine why she didn't attend. I mean it was she who set the whole thing up!"

Conversation moved on to the Barry Doyle Show, and the latest audience figures.

"We hit all targets. Willie Jackson is gutted!" Barry laughed. "He doesn't know how much leaks out of his office."

"I have a feature on adoption that might interest you. Have a listen." Veronica pushed the play button on her lap top.

"Veronica, that's quite a story!" Barry enjoyed working with her. "And to think what I used to say about your production!"

"Let's not. We are doing fine now." She teased him. "So you are happy to run with this?"

"Oh yes. Very happy. Where did you unearth this lad?" Barry was used to Veronica following his leads and contacts for features and they both enjoyed the results of the network of the gay community and their many supporters, relatives and associates.

"Pure luck, as it happens." Veronica was absolutely honest with Barry Doyle as this was the basis of their working relationship. With others she would dissemble or tell whopping great lies if the need arose, but not with Barry.

The story was simple but intriguing. It concerned an adopted boy, now an adult who had discovered he was the son of a bishop, and mothered by the woman in the couple who adopted him. The young man, using the pseudonym John, found out by sheer accident, after his mother's death, when he came across a photograph of his adopted mother and the Bishop.

"Why would the Bishop hide the fact? He's an Anglican! He has no duty of celibacy. He wasn't even married!" Barry asked with genuine incredulity.

"And how could the mother have adopted her own child – unless there was some serious deception and considerable assistance from the adoption and social services!" Veronica was more intrigued by what must have been systemic corruption – for she was convinced the woman must have used bribery to cover her tracks.

"If you think the social are bad here just look at the record of English authorities when it comes to child protection!" The programme researcher, Emily Foster, added with rancour.

* * * * *

Creating Wild Fern Alley had been a collective effort by the residents of Montague Road, College Road and Crusaders' Lane.

Marianne and Thaddeus quickly engaged a wide range of people from the middle aged married South African couple, retired academics, a serving judge, two gay male couples and a lady doctor who lived with her psychoanalyst sister. In the past few months two new families moved into College road and their children played with the many grandchildren who were regular visitors. Around twenty of the residences housed students, most of whom were somehow surprised that Marianne had lived in the area when she had been a student – why would that common experience seem so strange to these young people? A senior conservationist lived beside Jack Summers and the adjoining house was occupied by a veteran feminist and her actor husband. The next home accommodated four young barristers. The corner was a block of flats that faced onto the unkempt garden of Mrs Wilson, a widow of eighty four.

It was Mrs Wilson who was most upset by the appearance of the three landlords Cobbles, McVeigh and O'Doherty. She was afraid that they would all be taken back to the days when the Alley was the haunt of drug dealers and teenage prostitution.

"Will we have to put back all the seating and plants? It is so peaceful now – and I like to hear the children playing in the alley." Her voice was trembling and there were tears in her eyes.

"Not if I have anything to do with it Mrs Wilson!" Marianne was becoming increasingly angry with the opposition from the property owners – which seemed to have no reasonable basis but was undermining the entire project.

* * * * *

Veronica had spent a lot of time with the feature on 'John' and edited the lengthy interview with help from Andrew Simpson after he had officially finished his shift saying she was the only producer who could tempt him into unpaid overtime.

"This is another brilliant piece, Veronica." Her favourite and the most competent of the audio engineers willingly gave up his own time to work with her and did not expect the full credit that she always gave. Veronica was still feeling inadequate in the world of digital recording and broadcasting.

"Thanks. Yes, I think it will work well. 'John' is very articulate about his feelings and he comes across as honest – which never fails to hit the mark." She was pleased with the finished package. "I do appreciate your staying on Andrew. It wasn't a rushed job but it really makes my life a lot easier."

"To be honest, I have had so much rubbish to deal with today that it has been quite therapeutic my dear." He smiled, nodded and rose to leave the editing suite.

"Thanks again."

Veronica looked at her watch, knowing it must be late, as her stomach was rumbling. She took out a chocolate bar from her handbag and gobbled it down quickly. Still, she needed proper food! On her way back to what she now called home she stopped for a quick meal in Botanic Avenue. Every bite was divine and her temperament was restored to good humour within minutes.

By the time she returned to Montague Road the light was fading. The autumn nights were drawing in and the air was cold. Veronica Pilchard thought about Margaret Beightin's proposal. Clearly it was phrased to disguise her good friend's charitable intention. Despite all her independence and self-sufficiency she admitted that it was a gracious offer and one it would be churlish to reject. Nevertheless Veronica was enjoying city life, even though her room was now packed with new possessions. She was not a minimalist sort of person. She resolved to have a look at the cottage and decide then, although the offer would not have been made unless the place was habitable. She'd let Margaret know this evening and thank her.

Thankful to be secure, behind the heavy front door of Marianne Kelly's house she went to her room. Opening her phone she sent a quick email thanking Margaret for the generous offer and asking when she could view the cottage. To her surprise Margaret replied immediately.

"You can take a look any time. Let me know when suits and I can take you from my home. If I am busy I'll leave the keys and directions for you in the usual place." They had an agreed secret hiding place for just such exigencies.

"Margaret, thanks. I am not in studio tomorrow. Would late morning suit?" Veronica pressed the send button. She undressed ready for a shower and stood under the hot water feeling the day's work wash away. Dried and in fresh clothes she felt more settled than she had been for her time in Montague Road – and unsure about returning to Glenbannock where Harry Pilchard was settling back home.

Her phone pinged, signalling of a new message. It was from Margaret. The two were to meet at two thirty the next afternoon.

Downstairs Veronica made her way to the sun room. As she lit a cigarette she looked around the garden and noticed that there was a light in Eliza Taunter's house. It was the same light from the same window as she had noticed early that morning. So Eliza had been there all the time. That was odd – in fact more than odd. What was she doing missing the disciplinary meeting if she was no more than a couple of hundred yards from the main building of the university?

Unable to contain her curiosity Veronica Pilchard determined to ask the professor that question – whatever pretext she required. She put on a coat and walked to the house next door. Finding no response to her banging on the door – just in case the doorbell was not functioning – she called out to Eliza but to no avail.

Chapter Four

Jack Summers found himself more in tune with Veronica Pilchard's detection methods than he knew to be proper and professional. She was often more lucky than far-seeing, but she got results. With the help of Lady Margaret Beighton she also often managed to get to perpetrators before the police. Jack was also increasingly irritated by the command and control culture of policing – which had promised so many changes with the peace agreement reforms but these had not been delivered. He willingly acknowledged that there were real and present threats to the police in Northern Ireland and from numerous sources other than those Republicans who begrudged the social and political changes in the twenty first century. He'd remained in the service in the hope that a community policing approach would have replaced the quasi-military methods of their work. Yet every summer the heated atmosphere of keeping the peace between the still-warring factions at sectarian interfaces and along the routes of contested marches emerged in violent upheaval – and many of his colleagues were injured in the pursuit of their daily work.

That year the marching season had been as bitterly disputed in Belfast as ever. Although many outlying towns and villages were now capable of celebrating the Twelfth of July with Eleventh night bonfires, and bands and marches on the Twelfth without violence, a hard core of the residents in the capital tenaciously stuck to the old ways. Like many others from rural stations he had been drafted in to watch if not regulate the brutal confrontations between those passionate about marching and those aggressively objecting to what they considered a desecration of their local community and places of worship.

Jack was now considering his future and possibly a future outside the police. His father had left him rather well off, as the only remaining son and heir. He had the house in in College Road, the estate George Summers had left, as well as his share of the former matrimonial home.

It was with these thoughts in mind that he answered his phone.

"Jack, its Veronica here. I am worried about Eliza Taunter. I think here's something wrong."

Jack found himself listening to her with interest rather than the usual impatience. Veronica Pilchard was a poor judge of character but she had a nose for trouble, and danger.

After hearing that Eliza had apparently been at home but not turned up for Sandy's disciplinary, that there was a light on in her house but that she was not responding he was of a mind to take Veronica's version at face value – risky as that was for him, a policeman. "You do seem to have a point. Come over here and we can discuss the options."

Surprised that Jack Summers was taking her seriously, instead of dismissing her fears, she grunted an affirmative. She left by the front path of Eliza's house, taking a right turn into College Road and walked the short distance to the Victorian terrace.

Jack stood at the open front door and welcomed her into the living room. She took a seat on the couch in the now familiar bay window.

"A glass of wine?"

"Thanks." Veronica said no more, trying to figure out why Jack was not his customary self – suspicious and dismissing her 'theories' as nothing more than interference and speculation.

"You're wondering why I believe you may be right?" His voice was neutral but his soft smile showed he did not doubt her.

"Yes. You don't normally accept my suspicions as true."

"Now I know enough about Eliza Taunter to understand that she would not have missed that meeting if she were on the doorstep of the university." He paused, handing her a glass of red wine. "And since she was the person making allegations about Sandy, she was obliged to attend." He took a seat facing her.

"That is quite true. What makes me suspicious is that I saw a man leaving her house early this morning. Her bedroom light was on then and it's still on!" Veronica watched him for signs of the habitual contempt in which the police held her. There were none.

"And you made a lot of noise but got no response." Jack was talking to himself, thinking. His brow knit in contemplation.

"I know it sounds absurd but I have had this sense of foreboding since this morning. Could be hormones but I think it's something more substantial." She was reluctant to ask him to break into Eliza's house and sat, silent, hoping he would decide that such a path of action was justifiable.

"So you want me to break in through the back door – again?" He laughed.

"Is there any other way to find out what's going on?"

"There are a number of other options but I'm feeling reckless tonight."

Veronica could hardly believe it! Jack Summers was going to break and enter on the basis of her hunch, without a trace of evidence.

"Leave the wine. We can finish it later." Jack stood up, grabbing a jacket and reaching into a drawer in the heavy wooden desk. "Just what we need!" He grinned as he pocketed the bunch of skeleton keys.

They made their way along Wild Fern Alley, walking at a steady pace. As curtains were closed and there was no-one out of doors they arrived at Eliza's back yard without being seen. Jack scaled the wall easily, unlocked and opened the door in the red brick wall to admit Veronica and closed it again. He remembered the key he had used in the liberation of Nicola Tebaldi and quickly gained entrance to the back of the house.

Once inside they stood in the darkness. Jack called out "Anyone there? It's Jack Summers."

His voice echoed up through an empty hallway. The place was in total silence.

"Should we look upstairs in the bedroom?"

"No, we will start here on the ground floor." He pulled on latex gloves and handed a pair to Veronica. "We aren't here. Right?"

"Fine by me." She was astonished that he was snooping with her – ~~flaunting~~ every rule in the police code of conduct – but did not say so. flouting

The door to the kitchen-diner did not give way as Jack pushed it. It was open but something was stopping it. Jack used greater force and the door opened to reveal a scene of horrific violence. Lying in a pool of her own blood Eliza Taunter was dead. A large kitchen knife was sticking out of her chest – probably having gone right through her heart. Shards of broken dishes crunched beneath his feet. The room was hot, because the oven was on and the door open.

"Don't come in!" He ordered in a gruff voice. "She's dead. I'll ring the police now. You stay well out of here – it's a crime scene."

The smell of blood wafting out from the kitchen caught the back of Veronica's throat. A wave of nausea hit her and she vomited into the umbrella stand in the hall. Feeling weak and dizzy she sat down at the bottom of the stairs.

News of a dead body, certainly a murder victim, reported by a serving policeman was sufficient to generate an immediate response from the local station. Within minutes sirens wailed through the nearby streets and a police car pulled up in Montague Road, followed soon after by a somewhat disgruntled pathologist. Dr Raymond Dwyer had been dragged away from a formal dinner at which he was the guest speaker – his topic being the grisly tale of how Dr Harold Shipman had managed to get away with so many murders.

* * * * *

Leo Richards had completed his business in Belfast. Assuming the persona of Peter Saunders he had flown in a private plane from Newtownards airfield that morning and was now preparing to board a flight to Toulouse with his forged passport and identity papers. He was a wealthy man and would not be returning to Ireland or Manchester again. Certainly he was not reappearing as Leo Richards, the man whose fingerprints were all over the scene of crime in Eliza Taunter's home.

Richards had escaped police detection when they looked for him for the kidnap of Nicola Tebaldi. He was confident that he would evade them again, although the murder of Eliza would concentrate minds considerably more. He rested easy on the short flight and arrived in the evening, taking a taxi to his new home. The long day, following a sleepless night in Eliza's bed above where her body lay, and the excess of adrenalin left him exhausted despite his happiness and newly established wealth.

When he finally arrived at his villa he was met by the sight of French police. Alarmed he nevertheless met them with apparent equanimity, and was relieved to learn that his coastal refuge had been burgled.

"Oh, I don't think they will have got much. Most of my stuff is still in storage."

The police went through all the usual procedures, warning that they could not guarantee catching the culprit. Peter Saunders assured them that he had full insurance and that he was not afraid to stay in a house with broken locks for the one night.

The older of the two policemen looked askance at this Englishman, knowing how territorial and materialistic ex-pats were. He wondered that this one was not remonstrating and making the usual racist comments about the gendarmerie. Turning aside to his partner he whispered "Probably trying to be the macho man!" He had taken an instant dislike to this Peter Saunders and viewed him with suspicion – all the more so as he seemed less than enthusiastic about giving them his fingerprints. He made a note of that fact in his report on their visit to the crime scene.

* * * * *

Margaret Beightin was a very welcome visitor at Cressida Colliers' home. She found Margaret such good company and always parted from her friend sensing herself somehow more positive and self-confident. This morning they were planning a pre-Christmas river cruise holiday.

"I am so pleased you want to travel with me, Margaret. Belinda never says as much but she makes me feel she is doing her duty by going on these tours."

Pushing down the desire to inform Cressida that daughter Belinda was a spoiled brat who took after her father, lacking the basic courtesies to which she and Cressida adhered without a thought. She cleared her throat, "Cressida, my dear, I hardly think it's a duty to accompany your mother on what are luxury holidays. In any case, you may be assured that I am delighted to have a companion – I've got to the stage where I am rather nervous of travelling alone."

"Margaret Beightin I find that hard to believe!" Cressida laughed.

"I was never as daring as people thought – not at school or later. I have always presented a brave front. Besides when you get to a certain age, or have a bit of a limp like me, strangers can see you as a soft target."

The housekeeper arrived with a tray of coffee and cake. "Thank you Scarlet. Please put it on the table." Cressida smiled at the forbidding woman, receiving no more than a grunt by way of acknowledgement.

When Scarlet had left, closing the door with a slam, Margaret turned to Cressida. "She's not the most friendly, is she? I take it that John hired her." Her tone was direct to the point of bluntness.

"Yes, he makes all those arrangements." Cressida smiled weakly.

"Tell me, did he get the Lebrocquy I heard him mention?" Margaret had her own agenda, quite apart from making holiday arrangements.

"Yes. He was very excited about it, though it's not for him – I mean he's acquired it for a friend." Cressida had not shown it but she did notice Margaret's conversational sleight of hand.

"How interesting. John is obviously a good person to have around. And did he manage to acquire any other great works?" Margaret asked in a deliberately friendly tone.

"Yes, and you would understand how important they are. Not my choice – as you know I prefer watercolours – but fine pieces." She smiled deferentially at her guest. "He got a John Luke painting and three by Conor."

"What a find!" Margaret was certain this confirmed the link between Sir John Colliers and the Stewart Gallery. "That will put him in a really good mood – and happy for us to go on holiday, I should imagine." She winked conspiratorially at Cressida.

"Oh yes!" she grinned.

The two women spent the next hour drinking coffee and deciding on the dates and details of the escorted trips they would choose from the vast number on offer during the river cruise. Each wanted to compromise for the sake of the other, and both were agreed that lengthy walking tours were not an option.

"I'd prefer to miss the long treks – no matter how important the cultural significance is." Margaret said, seeing Cressida's tiny frown at the six hour walking tour of Prague. "Wouldn't we have more fun at the Christmas Market?"

"Definitely." Cressida smiled gratefully.

"I mean we are going on holiday not an educational excursion!" Margaret laughed. "Do you remember our first school trip to Paris?"

Reminiscing about their teenage experiences they were both transported back to a different age, where girls were chaperoned and the world was a safer place.

As the clock struck twelve Scarlet interrupted to announce that Cressida was required for a planning meeting about a forthcoming banquet.

"Well, Cressida. I have really enjoyed our chat and all those ideas for our holiday." Margaret said truthfully. She was extremely fond of her browbeaten friend. "Do let me know when you have time for another chinwag. You always make me feel fearless." She said without exaggeration. Now she was sure she was right about the art business – whether or not it was fraud there was something underhand about Sir John Colliers' dealings.

Margaret Beightin left the Colliers' house with the intention of changing the circumstances for the longsuffering Cressida. She had ample time to construct her plans before her appointment with Veronica that afternoon.

* * * * *

More than a week had passed since the landlords first took a public stance in opposition to Wild Fern Alley. Thaddeus had found out that Councillor Cobbles had misrepresented the facts by claiming to have complaints about the restoration of the Alley confirmed officially.

Marianne contacted the local council asking that the communal bins be relocated as there were rumours of a rodent problem. It seemed that she was persuasive as the job was done by the end of the day. Although she was nominally the chairperson of the group and meetings were in her home she was eager to step back and let someone else take over.

Adam and Steve, the older and more settled of the gay couples agreed to take on publicity and the web site.

"Of course I can't be seen near any news people. My brother is head of news!" Adam asserted. "That would be a real conflict of interest! Steve can do that and I'll do the web page."

"I still think Marianne is the best person to do interviews but I am okay with organising this stuff." Steve was not hiding the fact that he was rather intimidated by the antagonism with the property magnates and overawed by television cameras.

"I am so angry with Brendan Cobbles and Shappie McVeigh that I will just come across as a maniac – and the way the last piece was edited I sounded like a fishwife."

Adam could not resist a little scorn. "Marianne, my dear, you did say what went out on air!"

"Now boys, settle down." Thaddeus James was acting as peacemaker. "I think our story is small beer after last night's events."

"True. At the same time I think we should press the point about keeping the gates locked. It really could be a big security issue." Adam regretted the gibe. "Marianne, I apologise."

"Apology accepted Adam. This is no time for us to fall out. Look how far we have come."

They were a select bunch that morning. The middle aged married South African couple, two retired academics and the judge had sent apologies, as had the GP Jane Spencer and her sister Imelda. Colleen, the senior conservationist sat beside veteran feminist Annabella Clark and her actor husband Jimbo. One of the four young barristers was taking notes and agreed to act as secretary from now on. Simon and Cal the newly arrived gay couple were eager to join in and volunteered for just about anything that needed done. The elderly Mrs Wilson offered to do what she could to help but explained that she knew nothing about the internet or computers.

After some discussion they agreed that there must be some underlying motive for the landlords' belligerence – though no-one could come up with a credible explanations.

"Actually, we are doing them a favour. Despite their opposition and the negative publicity we've improved the housing market – prices are going up here. That is surely to their benefit."

"Perhaps it's all about control. They do what they want and resent anyone they can't dominate!"

* * * * *

Veronica had woken at nine to the smell of bacon frying. The previous evening's nausea at the smell of death in Eliza's house had gone and she was now extremely hungry. She opened her eyes, confirming that she was not in her own bed. Her mouth was dry and she wanted a drink of water and a hot shower. Dressed in her underwear she saw her clothes folded neatly on an armchair opposite the bed. She was in a guest room in what was now Jack Summers' house.

"Veronica, breakfast's ready – take a dressing gown from my room and come on down." Jack shouted up the stairs cheerfully.

Happy to let Jack make decisions as she had barely regained consciousness Veronica drank from the water bottle on the bedside table and went in search of a robe from Jack's room.

"Right oh. Down in a minute." She croaked, clearing her throat.

Veronica Pilchard had been deeply shaken by the sight and smell of bloody murder – although in truth it was mainly the pungent rancid smell of blood that seemed to linger in her nose and mouth.

"Good morning Veronica. Bacon, eggs and fried bread – washed down with hot sweet tea – that's what you need after last night's crime scene." Jack spoke from experience. There was something about smell that permeated the darkest reaches of the psyche, holding a power to resist all forgetting. Somehow sights could be processed rather like television pictures. Smell could hang around one's emotions for considerably longer.

"Thanks Jack." She sat at the table overlooking a large back yard that had been carefully planted with shrubs and herbs along the pathway from the patio outside the glass extension to the back wall. The sun shone brightly into a large kitchen-diner.

Jack took a large plate of Ulster fry from the oven and set it down in front of his guest. "You need tea – coffee and cigarettes can wait until later." His tone was almost paternal as he poured the brown liquid into a china beaker and sat beside her. "Nico is away for a couple of days but he's staying on here until he gets a billet of his own."

"Okay" was all that she said for the next ten minutes as she tucked into the meal and drank two beakers of strong heavily sugared tea.

Jack had finished the same dish before he'd called Veronica and now sat drinking his tea waiting for her to come back to full animation.

"It's as well we didn't finish the wine." Veronica said as she pushed an empty plate away from her. "That was great, Jack. Thanks."

Deciding that their discussion of the brutal murder could wait for a short while longer he suggested she take a shower. They had more formal statements to make to the local police that day, and should expect a long morning ahead of them.

Standing under a steady stream of hot water and still digesting a substantial breakfast, Veronica felt a surreal sense of security and happiness. Of course she usually experienced a sense of bliss when she had eaten well, but there was something else. She'd lost that oppressive sense of foreboding. Jack's wisdom in making a cooked breakfast, and his consideration touched her. For the brief time in his kitchen she'd lost that sense of loneliness which had stayed with her since the day Harry had returned and told her he was buying their home. She'd carried the rejection and aloneness without realising it had become a permanent shroud of misery that never completely went away – except for the occasional moment with her mystery man Mitchell.

In his professional role as a serving Detective Inspector Jack had explained that Veronica Pilchard had reported serious concerns about a neighbour, and had not been able to get any response when she called – even though there was a light in a window. She had seen a stranger leaving the victim's home early that morning – which is why they had taken the liberty of entering the house. Given that the horrific sight and smell of such a brutal killing had caused Ms Pilchard so much emotional and physical distress the investigating officer had agreed that they should attend together and mid-morning rather than at the start of the day.

Seasoned as he was in the business of violent crime scenes Jack was nearly as shaken by the scene of crime as Veronica. He wanted them to have time to talk over their story, avoiding all mention of skeleton keys. He anticipated that the SOCOs would not have finished their work and that the evidence that Veronica could provide would be relevant – possibly giving the police their only lead.

* * * * *

Margaret Beightin had not yet mentioned her forthcoming visit to the Stewart Gallery to her friend Veronica Pilchard. Although eager to involve Veronica she felt it was more pressing to get her to move from Montague Road. If possible she could settle both issues satisfactorily that afternoon.

Margaret had left Cressida Colliers in the certain knowledge that the Stewart Gallery now held the paintings which Sir John Colliers had obtained so recently. What she couldn't understand was how Colliers had come into their possession and from whom they been procured. Although it was quite illogical she felt Veronica would somehow help her get to the bottom of the matter.

As she had some time before Veronica was due to arrive she set about some background research on Luke and Conor – and the known whereabouts of their work. She leafed through her collection of books on Irish and Ulster art finding much of the material superficial and subjective so she turned to the internet – only to be met by an overabundance of sites. Not one to be overwhelmed by such a challenge Margaret Beightin refined her search and found a small number of highly informative sights, saving the references including her favourites from a social network site on fake art and counterfeiters in the twenty first century.

She was feeling rather smug as she closed her ipad, pleased that an older lady with no training could get so much information in a relatively short search. It was now nearly two. She was hungry and went in pursuit of a quick lunch.

* * * * *

Veronica was confident that her responsibility for entering Eliza Taunter's home would exonerate DI Jack Summers from any sanction. She had been astounded that he had so readily agreed to break in. He seemed to be a changed man since his father's death.

The policewoman who took her statement was DI Emily Brown. A suitably senior officer for such a serious investigation she knew Veronica's name from the radio.

"You produce the Barry Doyle show, don't you?" She introduced the topic as an ice-breaker as she had found witnesses to murder were often quite distracted when asked for evidence.

"Yes, Barry and I go back a long way – and we weren't always on such good working relations." Veronica smiled. "He is a consummate broadcaster so I was grateful to team up with him." She paused, sighed and continued "However, I am here today for other reasons. How can I help?"

"Just tell me why you were concerned about your neighbour and what you saw."

Veronica did not put a tooth in it. She described Professor Eliza Taunter as she saw her – a bit of an imposter. She went through the story of how Eliza had made serious allegations of misbehaviour against her student Sandy Hughes but had failed to attend the disciplinary hearing – although she appeared to be at home. There had been a light on and a stranger leaving the house early in the morning.

"I know it sounds ridiculous but I had this gnawing sense of trouble brewing all day long. Anyway by the time I got home that evening I decided I'd call on Eliza. There was a light on upstairs but I got no answer so I rang the doorbell and hammered on the door and shouted. Since I got no response I rang DI Summers. He is a neighbour and I wanted his advice. I told him I thought something serious might have happened to Eliza and we went in."

"Can you describe this stranger who left the house?"

"Not really. It was a man – about six foot, maybe taller. It wasn't quite light so I didn't get a good look at him. He was carrying a large bundle, a square parcel." Veronica stopped. "Now that I bring it back to mind, the bundle was wrapped in material, not paper, as it flapped like cloth in the breeze as he opened the front gate."

"Let me put it another way. Why were you suspicious about a man leaving the professor's house? Might she not have had male visitors or a boyfriend? She was divorced and living alone."

"Not Eliza. I haven't been at Marianne's for long but I got to know quite a lot about Eliza Taunter – apart from having her on the Barry Doyle Show. She was not hospitable. She never had visitors. For her entertainment was a seminar or conference where someone else did the cooking and paid the bills." Veronica knew this was a very unflattering picture and could see the policewoman's eyebrows raised in disbelief.

"DI Brown I am telling you the truth as I see it. It would be a lie to say that I thought Eliza was a pleasant, honest or sociable person – she was not the friendly type. That was why I thought it suspicious to see a man exiting after what might otherwise look like a one-night stand."

"Your candour does you credit Ms Pilchard."

"Oh do call me Veronica. I am a very direct sort of person. It goes with the territory. Broadcasting is not for the faint hearted."

"Well, Veronica, this stranger will almost certainly have left some forensic evidence behind. If it is there our SOCOs will find it."

"I wish I could tell you something of greater help. I did not like Eliza Taunter but no-one should ... I mean that shouldn't happen to a dog. And actually I was going to apologise for having set her up on Barry's show – she did make an ass of herself." Veronica finished with a glum contrite expression.

DI Emily Brown was impressed with Veronica's statement, uncompromising and brutally honest as it was. She stood up and held out her hand, "Thank you Veronica. I will have this typed up and you can sign it before you leave. It should not take long."

Veronica shook her hand. "I am happy to wait for as long as it takes. And if I think of anything – even the tiniest detail – I will report it immediately."

"Good, people do remember small things but often don't come back to us."

Sitting alone in the evidence room Veronica checked her phone. It was not yet midday and she had plenty of time to make her meeting with Margaret.

* * * * *

Jack Summers sailed through his formal interview about the murder of Eliza Taunter. The victim was now referred to by her given and surname – without title or honour. DI Emily Brown had delegated the task to her sergeant, knowing that Jack had an exemplary record and was a witness rather than a suspect in this murder case.

DI Summers went through the details in a precise tie-line. He reminded the officer that Eliza Taunter was of course known to the police due to the kidnapping of the young Italian Nicola Tebaldi who had been incarcerated in the basement of her home in the recent past. Although the culprit had not been found, police in Belfast and in Manchester knew him to be Leo Richards, the victim's former husband.

Veronica Pilchard, who was a known and trusted supporter of the police had expressed serious concern and provided good reason for suspecting foul play – and had come to him about the matter. He had gone with her to investigate.

"And you know what we found. In fact at this stage your SOCOs and forensics people will know a lot more than I do."

Jack paused and looked straight into the face of the interviewing policeman. "I could add the few details that Veronica had told me – about seeing a stranger leaving the house early in the morning. However, that would be hearsay. Presumably the victim was dead well before then."

"Quite. I think DI Brown will have that covered."

"Is there anything else I can add?" Jack had carefully avoided mention of the method used to gain entry to Eliza's home.

"No, DI Summers, I think that is all. Thank you I will have this typed up for you to sign." He looked at Jack and smiled, "And quickly. I don't want to keep you hanging about, Sir."

"As long as it takes, I don't pull rank, Sergeant, but thanks." Jack was contented with himself and quite sure Veronica would have avoided any mention of their breaking into Eliza's. As he thought about it he realised that he didn't care. He should have been concerned as this was a breach of conduct but he felt indifferent about that.

Waiting to sign his statement Jack checked his phone to find a short text from Veronica – "All done. C u later. VP"

He replied "Fine let me no where + when. J"

* * * * *

Sir John Colliers was in splendid form. He had the paintings in his possession and Frederick Stewart was about to arrive to take possession of them with at least one prospective buyer other than secretary of State Clive Heedon. Stewart was less than forthcoming about this other client but Colliers was not concerned so long as large sums of money changed hands in the near future – thus repaying his considerable investment handsomely.

When Cressida asked if she could take the pre-Christmas river cruise he hardly listened to a word she said. Wrapped up in a dream of greater riches than he had ever known, and the prospect of a continued source of lesser but still profitable fake art – coming on stream at discrete intervals – he looked surprised when his wife said, "John, I was asking about my taking time for a cruise – in December. Is that agreeable with you?"

"What? Yes, fine." He almost said 'whatever'.

"Good, then Margaret and I shall book our places this week." Cressida was hurt by this snub, eyeing a husband who had become more cold and distant with every year. "And I shan't have to impose on Belinda this time."

"Good, yes my dear. That will be fine." He waved her away as if she were some bothersome underling.

Cressida swallowed, feeling offended but a new-found anger replaced what would usually have been meekness. He was simply rude! Oh how she appreciated her dear friend Margaret. Her honesty was direct and even blunt but never boorish or offensive like John's or Belinda's. She drew herself up to her full height, breathed in and relaxed before starting a conversation.

"John, I can see you are spell-bound by these new acquisitions. Humour me and tell me about this windfall." There was an air of suspicion and resentment about Lady Cressida Colliers that her husband simply could not see – from the great elevation of his status as President of the Royal Society.

He turned to her, with a surprised look on his face. "They are not watercolours, my dear. They are paintings by Louis Lebrocquy, John Luke and William Conor. They are masterpieces, although as you will understand they are from very different stables."

Colliers proceeded to lecture his wife on the subject of the painters – sounding more like a used car salesman than an art buff and she indulged him for a full ten minutes.

"Indeed. That is impressive! So how did you come to get hold of them?" Cressida was asking the questions that she correctly guessed Margaret might ask. She had not been entirely fooled when her friend Lady Beightin had brought up the subject of the pictures quite out of context.

"Good luck and good contacts my dear. Clive Heedon knows this fellow Leo Richards and put him in touch with me. I met him first, saw documentation and agreed a negotiated price. After that his representative, Peter Saunders brought the product." He paused savouring his choice of word, product.

Cressida thought the term singularly inappropriate but smiled. "So this Mr Richards is not from here?" Her voice was laced with feigned sugary innocence.

"Gracious me, no!" Colliers looked as his wife. Thick was the word that sprang to mind. When he had married her she was a slender young thing but age and childbearing had thickened her waist – and seemingly her brain by the sound of her at that moment. "Actually he's English but he has retired to the South of France to pursue his artistic interests. I will be keeping in touch with him."

Cressida was concentrating hard to remember every detail – which she would note down and pass on to Margaret. "Well, you are a man of substance John, and I am sure Mr Richards is fortunate to have come across you." She turned and left her husband to his venal reveries.

In her own room she took out her gardening diary and penned in the names of the painters and the names Leo Richards and Peter Saunders.

* * * * *

Nicola Tebaldi was looking for a more permanent residence now that old George Summers had died and his summer-time house sitting had come to an end. He appreciated the fact that Jack was allowing him to stay on in the interim.

"Thank you Jack. I will pay you rent of course."

"Nico, you certainly will not! You are practically family after all the years you were here for my father!" Jack still could not use the word Dad without getting very emotional.

"Giorgio was a wonderful man Jack and treated me like family."

"And what about your own family, Nico. Aren't you going to visit your grandparents before teaching starts?"

"My teaching has all been rearranged, so I guess I do have time for a few days off. I really should go and see them."

A day later Nico was beginning his journey to his grandparent's farm just outside the village of Poggiduomo, near Verona.

He arrived to a tumultuous welcome and an unexpected reception for half the population of the village.

"Bravo Nico! Bravissimo Nico!" the small crowd roared as he came through the gate of the farmhouse.

"We shall have to call you Salvatore from now on! The saved one!" The local priest stepped forward.

Nonno Tebaldi embraced the young man. "Ciao Nico we are so pleased to see you really are safe."

"Mario, I told you the Lord would look after him." Nico's grandmother smiled indulgently and hugged her precious grandson.

"Olivia I had to see with my own eyes – but now I have, thank God!" There were tears in the old man's eyes.

The young man's confusion was obvious to all.

Olivia Tebaldi spread her hands outwards and up to the sky. "Nico, did you think we didn't know? I go to the Library for news of Belfast – and we read all about your kidnap and miraculous release."

There was a loud cheer and a round of applause from the assembled villagers.

"Now we can celebrate!" Mario Tebaldi gestured to the long tables set out for a feast of thanksgiving.

Over the next two days Nico spent time talking to his grandparents and listening to them. He told them about Veronica Pilchard and confessed to asking her for a cigarette, to Olivia's disapproval.

"Olivia he was lucky to get out alive. Forgive the boy a small sin."

They talked about the future prospects for Nico and themselves.

Mario was too old to farm and too frail to manage even the family allotment. Olivia was spritely for her years but was also keen to make changes to their daily lives.

"I am thinking about selling the land to a developer. These days there are few jobs in Italy – even in the Veneto – and fewer young people prepared to stay on the land."

"Where will you go?" Nico could not imagine his grandparents being anywhere else other than the farm where he had spent most of his childhood.

"Olivia thinks we should get an apartment. So we will be moving away from Poggiduomo."

"Will you not miss all your friends and neighbours?"

"Nico, you forget how old we are. Almost all my friends have died in the past few years. We go to mass and see friendly faces but we are mostly alone. We have each other."

"Before you sell the farm will you visit me in Belfast? I would like you to see where I am – that it is safe and I want you to meet the lady who saved me."

Seeing his grandfather hesitating he added, "I know a lovely woman who speaks a little Italian and has a beautiful home where you could stay – just beside where I am now." Nico planned to get accommodation of sufficient size to offer them a more permanent home – though whether or not they would accept was another matter.

Olivia Tebaldi had been listening, without interrupting, as the two men talked. She knew Nico was planning something – he was as transparent as he'd been as a young boy when he first came to live with them.

"Nico, tell us about the journey. We have never been outside Italy. How do we get to you and how long will it take?" She asked as if she was not fully aware of how to make the journey.

"If you come before the end of October you can get there from Verona airport and it takes just three hours or so to get to Belfast. There I will be waiting for you with a car."

Smiling, as if she had heard some new information – since she already knew all these details through the library and internet – she nodded. "That sounds simple enough. What do you think Mario?"

"From here it would take us three hours to get to Bassano by bus!" Mario was taking his lead from granny Tebaldi, understanding that she felt they should indulge Nico.

"And there's no car to meet us and no Nico in Bassano!"

"Then we shall come to Belfast and Nico." Mario clapped his hands to his grandson's delight.

* * * * *

Eliza Taunter's next of kin were her parents. They were informed of her death and the unfortunate circumstances by the police. As they had never been to Belfast and knew no-one from there, they were more than a little apprehensive about travelling to a former war zone where English folk were often unwelcome – at least from what they understood. Eliza had never invited them and they had never wanted to visit.

Now Gary and Stacey Taunter were obliged to do their parental duty, coming to Belfast to make funeral arrangements for their estranged daughter; relieved that her body had been formally identified by a local policeman. Eliza had rarely seen them over the years, keeping her parents as far away as possible. They were solid working people who voted conservative, celebrated royal births and anniversaries, and knew their place in the social order. They thought of themselves as good citizens but of course they were not bookish like Eliza and therefore were beneath her. They would say they were proud of her but in truth they were thankful of that distance and relieved to be rid of the dramatic scenes she so regularly created.

Since the body was to be released after a post mortem examination had been completed they willingly agreed to have the remains collected by the nearest reliable undertakers – as recommended by the police liaison officer. They also took advice about modestly priced accommodation and settled for staying for a flexible number of days with Marianne Kelly.

Gary and Stacey Taunter arrived with hand luggage only, hoping to conclude their duties as soon as the funeral was over. Marianne was able to trace Eliza's solicitor through the estate agent who had sold her the house – a sale that was very much to Eliza's advantage, since she convinced the elderly Mrs Stock that it was only worth the pittance which she was offering. Eliza was as unscrupulous in her business affairs as she was in matters scholarly – although Marianne did not consider her parents needed to hear that.

Gary Taunter was eager to end their stay as quickly as possible and without seeing the house or taking anything it contained he put it on the market for immediate sale. Despite being informed that it required cleaning and some repair he told the agent that the sale price was to reflect that.

"I simply want to leave all this unfortunate business behind us. As you can imagine my wife is distraught by all this …"

Embarrassed by the possibility that a grieving parent might break down in the middle of his offices the leading partner in Sells and Company he cut in, "Quite so Mr Taunter. I will see that our people take care of everything."

* * * * *

Margaret thought the cottage she had inherited provided the perfect inducement to extract Veronica from Montague Road and the life of an itinerant. She'd heard Marianne Kelly on the radio and was shocked by her tone and manner. The woman was common and such a harridan! How could Veronica live there! She would not tolerate that situation for a moment longer.

The bungalow was on the outskirts of Glenbannock, built on a hill above the church some hundred yards outside the thirty mile limit. Margaret drove them both to their destination with desperate hopes of extracting Veronica from a vagrant existence in Belfast. As they arrived the sun emerged from a cloudy sky. Margaret parked a short distance from the front door.

"We are at our journey's end." Margaret held out a small bunch of keys pointing to a large mortice one. "That's for the front door. You have a look for yourself. I'll follow you after you've had time to get the feel of the place." She smiled affectionately.

The house was bathed in autumnal sun, with a picture book cottage garden and picket fence at the front. Veronica was enchanted. The house was modest but had been modernised and Margaret's cleaner Molly Biggins had been in to air the place, clean and dust every room. She had even brought flowers from Margaret's garden which Veronica recognised in the upstairs landing table. Even the heating had been turned on. Although it was not a large establishment it seemed so spacious after living in one room for the best part of a month.

When she had inspected every room she stood in the landing, enthralled by the enclosure that was the back garden. Rhododendrons and Japonica had grown over the decades to make a tall thick blanket of hedging – protecting the house from the prevailing winds and giving almost total privacy from the nearby road. How could she refuse such an offer?

From below Margaret called up the stairs, "Have you seen enough?"

"It's fantastic, Margaret. It is just picture perfect. I love it!" Veronica was like a schoolgirl excited at the prospect of a new adventure.

"So you would consider taking it on for a while?"

"Absolutely!" The muscles on Veronica's face had lost their strain and the worn-down expression she had borne that morning had disappeared.

"Delighted to hear it. You can move in as soon as you like." Margaret reminded herself that this was not to appear like an altruistic hand out and smiled. "We can sort out finances later. In the meantime can I ask a favour of you?"

"By all means, ask away!"

"I want to go back to the Stewart Gallery and I want you to come with me. I can brief you on what to say to sound like an expert."

"I'll need a briefing – but yes I'll come with you. When do you want to do this viewing?"

"Could you make this evening?"

Veronica did not say she'd have preferred to move into the charming cottage because she was so grateful feeling sure that Margaret was making the offer to get her out of bed-sit living. "Why not? I'm free."

"Good. Why don't we have a bite together and I'll tell you what my thoughts are?" Taking on the role of the ebullient but still supercilious Lady Margaret Beightin, she replied to the invitation to view the paintings on sale at the Stewart Gallery with Veronica's phone.

Unfortunately Veronica lit a cigarette in the garden and Margaret's face darkened. "Veronica, I thought you had given up smoking!" Her voice was high pitched and accusing. She was suddenly overcome with anger. "If you are going to stay in my cottage you cannot smoke. You do realise that!" She snapped.

Veronica Pilchard was not a woman to be bullied. She was anxious to move into a place of her own but not that keen to leave Wild Fern Alley – and now that she had experienced the sharpness of Margaret's domination for the first time she thought again. "Steady on Margaret! It is not a crime." Margaret frowned.

* * * * *

On his return to Belfast Doctor Nicola Tebaldi was suddenly in demand at the university. He was the only person who was capable of taking over Eliza's teaching and supervision commitments at a week's notice. Assistant Dean Reynolds shed no tears at the news of the professor's untimely death. However, replacing her immediately was now his top priority.

Returning to College Road and Jack's house Nico was summonsed to meet Reynolds to discuss 'his prospects'.

Nico was held in good favour as both a researcher and teacher, as the Assistant Dean knew having already consulted the head of the School of Law before their meeting. His research and publications made him the perfect contender as her replacement – at least temporarily. Reynolds had a list and timetable of all Eliza's teaching and supervision obligations which lay on his desk as Nico entered.

"Good morning Doctor Tebaldi. Please take a seat." Reynolds did not pretend to any distress about the loss of Professor Taunter. "Very unpleasant business altogether but I have my responsibilities, as you will understand. I have to find someone straightaway to undertake her commitments. Would you consider taking on this?"

Reynolds handed Nico the timetable of lectures, seminars and supervision sessions for the coming semester. He continued, "Now I gather that you are more than well acquainted with the professor's area of expertise and that your record is exemplary, which is why I am taking this unusual course of action. Would you consider taking on these teaching and supervision duties?"

"Thank you sir." Nico carefully read the list of tasks, calculating how much of his time it would require. He did not make an immediate reply and Reynolds coughed.

"Of course, someone can take on your post-doctoral obligations – I have spoken to the head of the School of Law and that can be easily arranged."

"That makes it more feasible." Nico was astounded at the speed of change that was being proposed. He felt sure he could do as good a job as Eliza but he was not a professor.

"As you know the university has very strict equality policies when it comes to appointments. However, there is no problem about arranging a temporary contract." Reynolds cleared his throat. "And once a person is doing very particular tasks and in a specialist area they are frequently the chosen candidate, when a post becomes vacant."

"I do understand the importance of those policies sir." Nico could hardly believe what he was hearing – if only by implication. This offer was of stratospheric promotion. "I do believe I could undertake these duties – although I would make minor changes to some of the modules, if that is permitted."

"By all means, Doctor Tebaldi. By all means." Reynolds' relief was visible. "You would be doing me and the university a great favour if you could step into the breach!"

"Where would you like me to start?"

"If I might ask yet more of you, Doctor Tebaldi, you could start with the professor's office. I am informed that her parents wish to donate her writings and books to the university." He coughed, "And, to be blunt, the Library does not have the space for these items." There a hint of distaste in his tone.

"I quite understand, Sir. In fact it would help me considerably if I could access her teaching materials."

"Now, I have taken the liberty of having personnel draw up a contract," he smiled, "in the hope that you would accept my offer. I think you will find the remuneration satisfactory."

"I will liaise with the School Manager about the details, sir, and start preparation today."

"Oh, in case I was not sufficiently clear. You are to take over Professor Taunter's office."

Nico left the meeting with Assistant Dean Reynolds in a state of euphoria. He was being offered the chance of a chair! As he strode across the quadrangle he jumped in the air and kicked his heels together. He was actually quite confident about teaching these courses and was well aware of the topics Eliza's students were researching.

His time in personnel was equally gratifying, not least as he was being offered a salary double his current income – to be reviewed after three months. The personnel officer was clearly pleased for Nico.

"I am not sure if this is official yet, but I may as well tell you – in the strictest confidence of course. The post is to be advertised next month." He winked mischievously.

"How interesting!" Nico's said with a grin that spread right across his face.

* * * * *

The two women ate together at a bistro in Belfast city centre and Margaret told Veronica her thoughts on a probable art scam. Cressida had phoned Margaret to let her know what Sir John had said about procuring five paintings and Margaret was now certain there was a link between Colliers and the Stewart Gallery.

Margaret explained to Veronica. "I heard John Colliers on the phone mentioning Lebrocquy – he's a very important painter, sadly dead since 2012. That's why I went with you to the gallery before. Now a Lebrocquy has miraculously come on the market – so soon after I asked Frederick Stewart about the possibility."

"Yes I remember you talking about that."

"Well, not only has Stewart now got a Lebrocquy, but he also has some other paintings I am going to view. By more than mere coincidence they are by the same artists as the paintings Colliers has recently acquired – Cressida listed the artists for me." Margaret left time for the idea to take root in Veronica's impenetrable but sharp mind – hoping she would have some of her own thoughts on the matter.

"The Stewart Gallery will take its whack of course." She paused and looked at Margaret. "You know about the art world, Margaret. Tell me about Sir John Colliers and his pals."

"I think he's a pig! He looks like a pig and acts like a pig! I have known Cressida since we were at school and I am very fond of her. He runs their home like a – oh I don't know, but he has worn her down over the years. Anyway Cressida and I are going on a cruise together and it was when we were making plans that I heard him discussing Lebrocquy. She phoned me this morning and I gather he took possession of a bundle of pictures very recently."

The word bundle struck Veronica as an odd way to describe a collection of paintings. She made a mental note without interrupting her friend.

"I think he has passed the pictures on to the Stewart Gallery – which is why I am pretending to have a few spare million and want to buy the Lebrocquy."

"Who else would there be that would have that interest and that amount of money?" Veronica was speeding ahead, assuming that if the gallery handled art that cost so much there must be at least some very wealthy clients in the background.

"I imagine Clive Heedon would have an interest. He is also a pig but an extremely wealthy one!" Margaret recalled the after-opening dinner with some repugnance. "Politics is virtually a side line for him. He is sufficiently well off that he needn't work at all."

"Now that is extremely interesting." Veronica's face showed she was mentally typing up notes on her computer. "Would it be wise to mention his name when you are doing the viewing?"

Margaret ignored the fact that one does not 'do' viewing and smiled broadly. "I think that's a very good idea – after all I have met the man."

Armed with a briefing on local watercolourists – for which Lady Beightin's unnamed escort would show a decided preference – they left for the Stewart Gallery.

* * * * *

Eliza's funeral was as strange as it was sad. Her parents knew none of the people who attended. Marianne and a handful of residents whose homes backed onto Wild Fern Alley came to pay their respects, along with Veronica and Jack. The university was represented by Assistant Dean Reynolds. Nico attended out of a sense of duty, as rural Italians always came to funerals in their locality. The news of Eliza's murder had been in all the press and media, prompting Flags protester Dwayne Butcher to show up, awkward among a small crowd of liberals, pinkos and lefties as he saw them.

Veronica was the only face he recognised and he was grateful when she nodded to him as he came into the crematorium.

The service was taken by a man of the cloth who had never met the godless professor and who was none the wiser after speaking to her parents. Assuming that he was in the presence of highly educated and scholarly people he pitched his sermon on humility directly at them.

"Pride is a great sin. We are all equal in the eyes of God!" His voice rose and fell in a manner that singularly failed to impress the modest congregation.

He continued for some fifteen minutes on the importance of simple faith – quoting parables, often mistakenly, and drawing conclusions about the nature of humanity and the superficiality of the modern world.

Relieved that his droning harangue had come to an end, none of the supposed mourners sang *Abide with Me* with any enthusiasm. Gary and Stacey Taunter did not stay to shake hands with any of the people they assumed to be mourners. Departing for the car park no-one could miss the final indignity for Eliza Taunter. While one could justify her leaving this world in the cheapest coffin available on the market, it was difficult to defend the choice of the sole floral tribute. A tiny bunch of violets in a white china vase was all that to be seen – begging the conjecture that Eliza's miserliness was inherited from her parents, genetically or otherwise.

Out in the fresh air Veronica lit a cigarette as soon as was decently possible. She hated funerals. They created a profound turmoil when they were for someone for whom she had cared and a profound disgust on the rare occasions when she was attending out of a sense of obligation.

Jack had been silent for the duration of the ceremony. He'd watched Veronica closely noticing her discomfort. Now he cleared his throat, "Why did you come? It obviously annoys the hell out of you."

"It's the God-botherers as much as anything. Can't stand all the cant and humbug! I suppose I felt sorry for the parents – at least until I met them. Aren't they just horrible?"

"Maybe they are in shock. Who knows?"

"You sound like a police counsellor now, Jack!" She laughed. "Anyway I'm starving. Fancy a bite to eat?"

In the distance they saw Gary and Stacey Taunter getting into a taxi with their luggage, presumably going to the airport.

No-one grieved for Eliza Taunter.

* * * * *

Chapter Five

The SOCOs had found very little evidence at the murder scene, other than fingerprints and the foul smell remaining after Eliza's body had been removed. Her phone records showed no proof of visitors, expected or otherwise. There were no signs of a break in. The only indications of violence were in the kitchen where there had been a struggle and the victim had been stabbed – by her own kitchen knife by all appearances. It was difficult to determine the exact time of death because of the heat of the kitchen where the oven had been on at a high temperature and the door had been left open. The approximate time was late evening.

Veronica's statement was the only confirmation that anyone other than Eliza had been there – apart from the obvious fact that someone had killed Eliza Taunter. All the evidence was carefully stored but none of it gave detectives any clue as to who might have perpetrated the crime.

The case was a complete mystery without leads of any kind. DI Emily Brown was certain that it was some kind of domestic but would have to admit defeat when they turned up no leads to follow.

* * * * *

Lady Margaret Beightin arrived at the Stewart Gallery with the same friend as before, Frederick Stewart noticed. He wondered why someone who had the resources to buy a Lebrocquy did not appear expensively dressed, and sported nothing resembling costly jewellery – even though bling and mink were not the usual dress for his clients – and she came on foot. He greeted the lady warmly, having calculated his commission with mercenary anticipation.

"Good evening Lady Beightin!" He spoke with careful diplomacy. "I have the works ready for you."

"Thank you Mr Stewart." Margaret really disliked this sort of obsequiousness and responded in a curt tone of voice. "I am looking forward to the viewing."

Veronica kept silent as they were ushered into a large room off the main gallery space. Walls, ceiling and floor were painted a pristine white. The light was artificial, but modulated rather than intense. Stewart pressed a button, and there was a faint whirring noise as one of the walls slid gently back revealing the Lebrocquy.

Margaret gasped in admiration and Stewart smiled indulgently – she was showing a real art lover's interest! The core of the picture was no more than forty centimetres by thirty, set against a background of white with a subtle but faint rainbow of detectable colours among the thick impasto. It was the face of a middle aged woman, with magnetic eyes, a round soft mouth and an abundance of black hair tied in the French knot.

Stewart knew better than to utter a sound. A client seeing a great work of art for the first time, which they wanted to purchase was like the intense gaze between two lovers – and not to be interrupted. He rubbed his carefully manicured hands.

"It is a work of great affection and respect. Who is the sitter?" Margaret was mesmerised. The painting seemed to be alive – just as in the best of Lebrocquy's work.

"It is Hortense – the woman who was the Lebrocquy family's housekeeper and child minder. She was with the family for some years and cared for the sons." He stepped back from Margaret to allow her to keep her fixed gaze on the painting.

"I have never seen it catalogued among his works." Margaret spoke more in curiosity than accusation. "Where did it come from?"

"Hortense died early this year and one of her children sold it to a buyer in France. I understand that she had needed medical care and had agreed that it should be sold to meet some substantial bills."

Margaret thought that this was plausible, although she suspected Frederick Stewart would not be above accepting something that was of doubtful provenance.

Seeing Lady Margaret had disengaged herself from the thrall that had captivated her Stewart nodded. "I can assure you, Lady Beightin that I have full documentation and a photograph of Hortense with the Lebrocquy family. This was one of his portraits of heads – like those better known of Joyce, W. B. Yeats and Francis Bacon."

"I have to say it is a remarkable painting. However, I think you might also arrange an authentication from the National Gallery."

Margaret knew that there had been a woman called Hortense who was almost part of the Lebrocquy family and felt sure the picture was genuine. "Now I believe you have some other works."

"Indeed I do!" Stewart almost bowed. They stepped back from the recessed space. He pressed the button and the white wall resumed its original position, covering all traces of the Lebrocquy. He showed the two women into a smaller room where five paintings were displayed against a linen covered wall.

"This is a John Luke – very typical." He cut himself short, fearful of seeming to patronise Lady Beighton. He stood back.

She examined the carefully constructed work, detailed in the same vein as a Luke but her instinct told her this was a forgery. "Interesting."

She was clearly not in awe of this as she had been with the Lebrocquy. Stewart cleared his throat and gestured to the adjoining walls.

"These are by William Conor. Full of the richness of rural Ireland." Again he restrained himself from his customary patter.

"Ah, these are very good!" Margaret turned to Veronica who had not spoken a word. "What do you think my dear?"

"They are really well executed, but I'd go for a Tom Carr sooner than a Conor." Veronica had remembered her briefing – though she took Margaret's word for it that what she was saying made sense.

"We have very different tastes Mr Stewart but my good friend has an expert eye." She smiled condescendingly at the art dealer. "She is fond of watercolourists – rather like dear old Clive." She hesitated and seeing Stewart was not reacting, added, "You and Clive Heedon are twins in that respect!"

"Ah you know Clive Heedon?" This got Stewart's full attention.

"We have met socially." Margaret said in a neutral tone. "I gather he owns a number of Carr pictures."

"I shall have to see to it that I find some of Tom's work for your friend – he was such a lovely man." Stewart gushed. "And you might also appreciate David Evans' work?"

"Oh, yes indeed. I think he shows a painterly eye and an exceptional perspective." Veronica was spot on, but running out of scripted lines.

"Well, Mr Stewart. This has been a most interesting evening's viewing. If you could obtain authentication I would be interested in the Lebrocquy. And I will give some serious thought to the John Luke – though not for myself – I have a nephew who would give his eye teeth for a good John Luke!" There was a twinkle in her eye and a mischievous pitch in her voice that Veronica detected immediately. She struggled to suppress a laugh. Margaret was at her most dazzling in performances such as this.

Margaret and Veronica left the Stewart Gallery without any contract being agreed, but still managing to convince the art dealer that he had at least one sale on his hands.

* * * * *

Details of Eliza Taunter's funeral spread among the clientele of the Golden Palace. Sandy Hughes whistled the tune of *Ding dong the witch is dead* as he swept the floor of Curl up and Dye – and although Desmond reproached him with a mocking "Now steady on pet" he joined in.

News of Nico's good fortune created much greater interest in the hairdressing salon, not least as Sandy knew Doctor Tebaldi would make a formidable academic adversary, but a fair-minded one.

Veronica sat listening to the chat, sipping a gin and tonic, indulgently.

"That's one of the great advantages of living in town – you don't have to drive." Desmond said as he teased her hair.

"This is heaven." Veronica surrendered herself to the magic of Desmond's talent, happy that he could reduce at least some of the signs of ageing.

As if reading her mind he whispered, "And don't do Botox my dear. The sad thing is that it only works for people who have no real wrinkles. I'd try it myself but I have seen the results – ugh! Not pretty."

"Ah, you mean Sammy at the Golden Palace!"

"Well, honestly, doesn't he look a sight now? And with that hair dyed blonde! A diseased daffodil! That's what they call him, behind his back."

"How? Can you read minds?" She asked wondering if Desmond really did have the psychic powers that he was rumoured to possess.

"Not psychic Veronica. I see it all the time – here and at the Golden Palace. One bad day in the company of young lovelies and the most grounded of people start to panic. Now you are steeped in the mire of enforced youth at the Beeb, so it is bound to get to you sometimes."

"Ha ha!" She laughed, feeing reassured if a spot embarrassed.

Ageing was an unpleasant reality for Veronica. She could detect the increase in the number and thickness of tiny hairs on her chin, and what might be euphemistically called laughter lines. She had investigated cosmetics for the mature skin on the internet which was a rather depressing search.

"Anyway, you won't believe this. Nico is looking at Eliza's house. It's up for sale and he is looking for a place of his own."

"Eliza's house? Isn't that a bit soon? It was a crime scene a week ago!" Veronica felt there was something just too insensitive about Eliza's parents leaving her home and office in the hands of complete strangers. "Didn't her parents even want to take something small to remember her?"

"Apparently not. The lead partner in Sells and Company is handling it all – but having real problems."

Desmond told Veronica that there were all kinds of rumours on social media about the house and even hard-nosed speculators felt it would prove hard to let out – and expensive to get into decent shape.

"Of course she bought from Mrs Stock – a great chum of my mother back in the day. Eliza got it for a good price and did nothing except remove the grab rails from the front of the house. It needs a huge amount of work done." Desmond exhaled through his teeth quietly expressing a degree of disgust. "Eliza took all the contents, some of which were valuable but gave her a pittance and Mrs Stock was old and confused and knew no better."

"I should think that's the last place Nico would want to live in!" Veronica recalled the young man's plaintive singing of Panis Angelicus and the traumatic state he was in when they had retrieved him from the basement.

"I think he has plans but he is being rather tight-lipped about it. He said he wants his grandfather to look at it when he comes to visit." Desmond gave a conspiratorial wink, adding, "And Nico wants them to meet you – the heroine who saved his bacon!"

* * * * *

Jack Summers had returned to duty after a short period of compassionate leave. Although he had not been away from Donaghdubh station for more than a couple of weeks, it felt as if he had been living in another world for the intervening time. Detective Chief Inspector Bill Adams greeted him, as the most senior officer and his boss.

"Sorry to hear about your father, Summers. It is always a shock no matter how elderly a person is when a loved one leaves us." Bill Adams was genuinely sympathetic, and typically unable to articulate an appropriate condolence with ease.

Jack nodded and said thanks. He went to his desk, eager to get into investigating whatever criminal business lay there waiting. He felt unsettled, and uncomfortable with the environment.

Discussion of the murder of Eliza Taunter would inevitably come up, although the crime was not on their patch – which meant that mention of Veronica Pilchard was inescapable. Jack knew DI Adams was far from a fan of Veronica – believing her to have put Lady Margaret Beightin in danger in her previous escapades as an amateur sleuth and a malign influence on a vulnerable lady. He could not understand how she was susceptible to trusting that shrew!

Jack had not met Margaret since she and Veronica had solved the murders of Matilda and Walter Muckle – and uncovered a paedophile ring that included a very senior member of his own police force – so he did not know that DCI Bill Adams was seeing her. Margaret was a fine woman whom he admired but much more worldly and self-sufficient than the DI supposed.

When the subject arose Jack announced that he'd heard a rumour that Veronica Pilchard was returning to Glenbannock. "Lady Beightin is renting her a cottage, so she will be safely out of the circulation and unlikely to be sleuthing in Belfast." As he spoke Jack was suddenly absolutely convinced that Veronica Pilchard and

Margaret Beightin would most certainly be at the centre of amateur investigations.

* * * * *

Marianne Kelly was not a woman who was easily intimidated but she knew that directly challenging property magnates brought the risk of reprisal if not actual danger. She was therefore suspicious when a second dead rat appeared at her front door.

Fortunately Marianne was usually the first person up in the morning, With the exception of Veronica Pilchard her guests rarely rose before eight in the morning. Taking the offending item to the communal bin in the Alleyshe spotted Thaddeus talking to Desmond, Adam and Steve. She took the opportunity of asking them if they had discovered dead rats around their homes or gardens.

"Oh my God no!" Desmond squealed.

Steve shook his head. "We've had nothing like that at all."

Thaddeus an early riser and often used his attic for painting in the silence of dawn. He looked at Marianne and asked. "Where did you find it?"

"On the front doorstep." She winced with disgust hold the plastic bag at a distance and tipping it into the bin.

"I saw Councillor Cobbles on the road this morning." He raised his eyebrows.

"That bastard!" Marianne cried out in anger. "I will put up a web cam and catch him if he does that again!" The knuckles in her tightened fists were white and her jaw was clenched.

"That would be advisable – and evidence." Thaddeus spoke with gravity. "I think we need the environmental health people out, don't we?"

"And look the solar lights have been stolen!" Adam chipped in.

The four stood nodding as one. Open hostilities wold be more easily dealt with than behind the scenes briefings and stirring up distrust among the residents' group.

* * * * *

Veronica wanted to move out of Marianne Kelly's home but she was not going to live in Margaret's cottage in Glenbannock. It was perfect but it was not her property and she would be beholden to – much less bullied by – Lady Beightin. She was shaken by the arrogant treatment, rankled that Margaret would try to browbeat her into changing her behaviour and her lifestyle. In fact it had come as an unpleasant surprise that Margaret had spoken to her in that manner at all. Veronica was beginning to doubt her self – she'd never imagined Margaret would turn her sharp tongue on her. Weren't they good friends?

Shocked at this unwarranted attempt to control her and offended by Margaret's suddenly changed attitude she had watched her carefully in the Stewart Gallery – wondering if she might be the next person to be subject to this high-handed routine. Saddened but determined to avoid unnecessarily falling out with one of the very few friends she had Veronica had spent the rest of the night trawling through rental sites until she found a couple of possibilities. By eleven o'clock the next morning she would have viewed both and decided.

Thinking about the options of town versus country she was not sure she preferred rural life. However, what had started as an exciting change from Glenbannock, and a clean break from her marital home and estranged husband was now wearisome. She missed the wide open skies of the countryside and found living in the university area when students returned constricting. She also acknowledged that she did not enjoy the simple life, with few possessions. Indeed as she packed her possessions – anticipating that she was going to buy or rent within days – she discovered her two suitcases were woefully inadequate to the task of carrying all the things she had accumulated in the space of less than a month. At the same time Veronica had become so involved in Wild Fern Alley and her new romance that she settled for trying to rent a small apartment there.

Behind the façade of energetic enthusiasm she was both indecisive and in low spirits. She liked the people she knew in Wild Fern Alley but was depressed about Margaret's behaviour. She braced herself for the day ahead and the possibility of their special friendship ending when she turned down the offer of the cottage.

Both places she viewed were pleasant but the better option was a ground floor flat that gave unto the Alley and was owned by Mrs Wilson, who lived in the top two storeys. Mrs Wilson was delighted that she knew and trusted her new tenant. They agreed a short term lease as Veronica was determined to get her own place eventually. Handshakes over, Veronica Pilchard strode into the city centre and the BBC with renewed independence and purpose. Postponing any prospective house purchase was freeing her up her time and energies – now focused on Wild Fern Alley. She went back to Montague Road feeling a stronger and happier woman.

Marianne was happy to have the room free as she had a full house now that the theatre season had started again in earnest and Nico's grandparents were due to arrive in a few days.

Veronica was grateful to her landlady. "I really must thank you Marianne. You have been truly hospitable." She did not add that she had been vulnerable and appreciated the friendly reception.

"My pleasure. You have been a most fastidious guest." She offered her hand and Veronica shook it, sincerely grateful for this friendship. "I know Nico's grandparents want to meet you so I expect we'll meet again soon."

"Yes, you have my contact details – and I'm not going far! Give them my number and tell them I can visit at a time that suits them." Veronica decided to try and improve her very basic Italian before meeting them.

* * * * *

Wild Fern Alley was again in the news but only because of press speculation that it was the entry point for the person who had murdered Eliza Taunter. Police were not commenting on the scant evidence they had and made the usual statements about following all possible leads.

At least two junior reporters were on permanent watch in the hope of getting a scoop. The fact that there had been no break in and that there had been no intruder in the Alley and back entrance to seven Montague Road did not deter the young newshounds.

Councillor Cobbles and Shappie McVeigh were deterred, however. They still retained keys to the gates but had kept away from the Alley since the murder. They certainly were not going to be found leaving the gates open and were regretting having started the rodent problem. Their plan to have the public access to Wild Fern Alley restored would have to be put on hold.

Brendan Cobbles could not tolerate this for long, which was why he'd deposited the dead rat at Marianne's door.

Thaddeus James was suspicious about why the landlords were so opposed to the collective improvement – as it was to their benefit as much as any of the residents – and he shared his concerns with Marianne and Johnny McBriar, the young barrister now secretary of their group. "Although they keep changing the reasons for their opposition the one consistent complaint is about access to the alley. Why do they want public access when they know if they are expecting deliveries and they have keys?"

* * * * *

DCI Bill Adams was shaving with extra care and dressing in is best suit for the evening's concert. Margaret Beightin had agreed to attend a Chopin recital in the Ulster Hall with him. He had not seen her in person since her Mediterranean cruise and the prospect of her company was exciting. He fiddled with his cufflinks – an action that reminded him how much he had taken his wife Brenda for granted. She had always done up his cufflinks. She was reliable and had his dinner ready at almost any hour of the night when he returned home. She kept the house clean, did the laundry and lived her life around his irregular hours without complaint. At first he had not missed her when she left him to go to the antipodes with 'that feminist woman'. These days he relied on a twice weekly cleaner, convenience meals and local laundry. Brenda still sent him regular emails and had offered a quick divorce if that was what he wanted. He procrastinated feeling somehow shamed at how events had turned out.

Struggling with the second cufflink he decided to change his shirt. Buttons would have to do!

He was displeased to hear reports that Veronica Pilchard was returning to his patch and therefore would once more become a regular visitor with Margaret Beightin. He had been delighted when she left Glenbannock and so ceased to be a threat to the dear lady's safety. He knew however that Margaret would either laugh at him or be angry if he said as much. Reluctantly he opted for avoidance, harbouring a silent resentment towards 'that damned woman'.

The thought of a cultured evening and the melodious strains of Chopin eased his mood. He went downstairs clutching the concert tickets and smiling.

* * * * *

Transforming the scene of Eliza Taunter's murder into an attractive property was quite impossible. Although the estate agent had sent in industrial cleaners number seven Montague Road was far from what a prospective buyer would want to see. In the space of not much more than a week rats had got in, so the rodent squad had to start the onslaught on the house.

Soft furnishings had to be removed leaving the place looking derelict rather than empty. The remaining contents were dusted and flooring cleaned. However, the appearance was still a gloomy one lacking all traces of homeliness.

Nico had asked to view the property once he realised that it was on the market for a reduced price. Calculating that he could take on this renovation project with some professional help, he could see its potential. He did not tell anyone that his aim was to have a place where his grandparents could settle with him to support them.

Mario and Olivia Tebaldi had been adoring grandparents to him and now faced an uncertain future as old age pensions had been one of the many casualties of the Italian recession, and their land would not necessarily fetch as much as they had lead him to believe.

Keith Sells was the leading partner in Sells and Company and dealt with the property himself, since Gary Taunter had made it clear that any cleaning costs, taxes or fees could be taken from the sale price. He had left instructions that the buyer could take the contents or Sells and Company could have them disposed of. Keith found this a peculiar request and guessed correctly that the family was not a close knit one. In fact he thought the father seemed shifty and came across as guilty. He did not share his opinion with the foreign young man who was about to view the property.

Opening the door Sells was relieved that the foul smell of murder had been eradicated. "You may wish to take a look around yourself Doctor Tebaldi or I can show you each room."

Nico had learned from regular childhood visits to the local market with his grandfather that maintaining silence and a poker face was an essential tactic in successful negotiation and if he was to put a bid in for this house it would take every penny that he had saved over the years. He sniffed. "I would appreciate you taking me around – that way you can point out the best features." His facial expression did not show enthusiasm or great interest.

"Indeed, that might be advisable. This home has enormous potential, although one does need to have some imagination at the moment."

As all carpets had been removed their footsteps echoed through the house. Nico could tell at a glance that the stairs and floor boards were hard wood and probably the original fittings as were the doors – albeit under layers of paint.

Sells made a point of listing every probable element of the original fittings, gesturing to cornices and cast iron fireplaces, and commenting that the three flights of stairs including bannisters were assuredly hardwood under the paint that masked their decorous glory. "And of course, Doctor Tebaldi, the wooden sash windows will make an enviable exterior when refurbished."

Nico nodded as Sells went through his spiel saying nothing, but watching to see if this professional was feeling slightly pressured. He was.

Sells had carefully guided their tour of the house so that the kitchen and basement were the last rooms to be seen – painfully aware that these had each been the scene of now notorious crimes.

Judging the moment perfectly Nico cleared his throat and said, "So this is the macabre scene of crime then?"

"Yes, dreadful business altogether." He was visibly uncomfortable. "You do understand that the vendor has left instructions that the contents can be left for the buyer or we can dispose of them. The choice is yours Doctor Tebaldi."

"Aside of the kitchen – which needs completely replaced – I might consider keeping some pieces. Of course there is the rewiring and plumbing work to do – and that's before the total redecoration."

Nico rubbed his chin, calculating that he could do much of the donkey work himself, but looking rather concerned.

The basement, which he recalled in intimate detail, had been scrubbed clean and was startlingly bright under harsh fluorescent light. He noticed a trap door in the bleach scoured wooden floor but averted his gaze, determined to leave a full examination until a second viewing, in the company of his grandfather.

Aware that he might be overdoing the strong silent type Nico offered a crumb of hope to the estate agent. "This is really a lot larger than I'd have thought. A useful space."

Grateful for a positive comment at last, Sells relaxed a little. "Indeed it is. And as you see there is a sizeable back garden."

Their viewing complete, they left by the front door. Nico had given the impression he desired – that of a person interested but with serious reservations. Now it was time to hook the bait.

"My grandparents are coming to visit in the near future. I would like to arrange another viewing with them, if that is possible."

"Oh, yes Doctor Tebaldi!" Sells was delighted. Nico was so far the only person who had shown any interest.

"Then I will contact you – if you are available on the 6th or 7th of this month."

"I will pencil in those dates and make myself available." Sells was now keen to find a buyer for the place and as quickly as possible – that house was disturbing and unnerved him.

Nico had sensed the man's uneasiness from the moment they had stepped inside number seven Montague Road. He found it thought-provoking since he was impervious to whatever Sells found disconcerting.

* * * * *

Cressida Colliers had made a note of the names of the two men who had assisted her husband in buying the paintings. However, she had not thought it relevant to mention these to Margaret Beightin – since she knew enough about art to make sound judgements about what she saw. Cressida was much more interested in booking their cruise.

Sir John Colliers was impatient to hear news of the as yet unnamed buyer of the Lebrocquy and, having had no communications with Frederick Stewart decided to pay the gallery an unannounced visit.

"Ah Stewart, just the man!" He pronounced as he entered.

"Sir John, how good to see you. To what do I owe this unexpected pleasure?"

"My desire to know the mystery client who has been viewing the paintings." Colliers spoke with a sharp tone.

"Oh, Sir John, she is not a mystery. Not a mystery at all!" Stewart sensed the hint of threat that Colliers so clearly intended to convey. Something in his obstinate nature wanted to prolong the anonymity of Lady Margaret Beightin but he understood Colliers and knew he had to impart this information. "It is Lady Margaret Beightin."

"Really? I had no idea she had that sort of money."

"I don't know about her financial standing but she was deeply impressed by the Lebrocquy!" Stewart spoke with relish at the memory of an enthralled Lady Beightin.

Since Colliers did not know about Margaret's financial standing either he changed the subject. "So is she going to buy it?"

"She wants an authentication from the National Gallery and I am arranging for that in the next couple of days."

"And, I take you will inform me of any progress – on that or the others." Colliers was giving an abrupt order rather than making a request.

"Oh, yes, indeed, Sir John. As soon as there is any movement you will be the first to know." He smiled obsequiously adding, "And she may also take the Luke."

Colliers turned on his heel and left without further comment. Something made him uneasy about Margaret Beightin's interest in these two paintings.

As he returned home he considered whether Cressida might have made mention of 'the product' to her friend Margaret. It rankled with him that she might also look for authentication on the Luke picture, as he had acquired it for a price that reflected its uncertain origin. It irked him more to think that his dim-witted wife was unknowingly interfering with his business. Colliers was keen that Lady Beightin held him in high regard in his quest for the prize of National

Governor of BBC Northern Ireland. He certainly did not want her having any suspicions.

Sir John Colliers was a man's man. He found the female sex dull by comparison and usually more interested in small talk than serious discussion. He preferred the sonorous tones of the male voice to the high pitched chatter of women. Of course there were exceptions, such as Margaret Beightin. Thinking over her potential wealth he wondered that he had not known about that before. Most people who are well heeled do not hide the fact but Lady Beightin gave every appearance of possessing a high social rank rather than an elevated financial status. He made a mental note to ask Cressida about that at dinner.

* * * * *

Jack Summers was now struggling with his workload. There was nothing to demand his attention beyond the odd petty crime in Donaghdubh. He was finding the command and control culture of policing more irritating by the day. Part of this was his inability to deal with his grief but he also had an underlying sense that his time in this job had passed its shelf life.

His mind was on detection, but not on the investigations on his desk. He was preoccupied by the apparently motiveless abduction of Nicola Tebaldi and the murder of Eliza Taunter. Both offences had been committed in the same house. Leo Richards had never been located and whoever murdered Eliza Taunter was as yet unidentified. He was sure there was a connection but could not figure out what linked the two crimes.

He knew he was being surly at the station and sharp with his colleagues. In his miserable state of mind he could not shake off the urge to resign. He had seen DCI Adams' expression of frustration and annoyance at his behaviour – knowing he was being given a wide berth because of his bereavement.

Today he was just going through the motions, taking statements about a minor burglary, cross examining two likely suspects from Donaghdubh – Billy Duff and Gerry White. He was so slapdash that he overlooked a cache of stolen items dumped at the back of a cupboard in Duff's house. It was Detective Sergeant Gary McClure who stirred him from his stupor.

"Jack, look what we have here!" Gary McClure had worked with Jack for years and knew this carelessness was totally out of character.

"Sorry – I was miles away. What is it?"

"Two phones and a handful of credit cards, plus some ornaments and jewellery." DS McClure held a black bin liner in his gloved hand.

"Banged to rights I would say." Jack Summers felt ashamed of his dereliction of duty. "Gary this is your collar. I'm not at myself at all."

Knowing that to be exactly the case but unwilling to say so Gary McClure responded. "The main thing is that we have this cleared up Jack."

That evening Jack wrote out his letter of resignation.

* * * * *

Mario and Olivia Tebaldi arrived in Belfast, driven by Nico from the airport to Montague Road and Marianne Kelly's house. The early evening was bright, clear and sunny and the elderly couple strained to see as much of the city as possible from the back seat windows.

Once greeted by their landlady and having deposited their luggage in their room they came downstairs to Nico.

"Shall we go out for a meal? Alberto's is a good Italian restaurant." Nico looked at his weary grandparents. "Or perhaps I could bring something if you prefer to eat here?"

Mario looked exhausted but laughed, "Alberto's must be good by the look of your face. What do you think Olivia?"

"It is a lovely evening. Is it far?" Olivia looked at her best shoes wondering if she could bear to walk further in them. Nico noticed this with a sideways glance.

"It's not far, but perhaps you should maybe change into more comfortable shoes. It will take us ten minutes to walk there."

"If you wait for me I will get my walking shoes." Olivia smiled.

Outside Nico watched them closely pleased his grandparents seemed to enjoy the walk.

"Fresh air! The aeroplane was very stuffy so this is just perfect." Mario chuckled.

"Alberto will be pleased to meet you – I told him I would bring you. And you will be understood in Italian."

"Senora Kelly speaks quite good Italian, Nico. Thank you for finding us someone we can talk to. Our English is not so good." Olivia seemed relieved.

"Nonna! Did you think I would leave you with foreigners who have no Italian?" Nico teased her. "I will make sure that I am with you, or Marianne or someone with a bit of Italian for every minute of your stay."

The three Italians were greeted with applause, cheers and a standing ovation by the staff at Alberto's. Alberto himself stood at the best table bowing to the visiting grandparents. "Please sit." He nodded and gave a wide grin, "This is a great pleasure Senor and Senora Tebaldi – a great honour. Your grandson Nico is a welcome customer at any time but especially this evening. We have heard about you both for so long and it is good to meet you at last."

All conversation was conducted in Italian to the delight of Mario and Olivia.

They dined on specialities that Alberto had prepared – briefed by Nico on his grandparents' favourite dishes. Wine from the Veneto region pleased Mario.

By the time they had finished their meal Nico ordered a taxi. His grandparents were ready for a short drive and a long sleep.

Alberto would not hear of payment for the meal. He blustered about the honour and respect of Italians. Mario enjoyed the pantomime and conceded.

"Thank you for your generosity. The food is superb – as is your hospitality Alberto."

Nico took his leave of them at ten, assuring them that he would return in the morning.

* * * * *

The Ulster hall was refurbished in 2009 and is home to the Ulster Orchestra. A Victorian music hall it is relatively small in comparison to the new concert venues. Its elaborate décor reflects the fact that it was built by a linen magnate at a time when Belfast was a great industrial metropolis – more significant than most of the large English cities. The architecture appealed to Bill Adams, with its sturdy stone and cast iron columned edifice. The rigid strictures of building in the 1860s gave him a sense of solidity, discipline and order.

Escorting Lady Margaret Beightin was a privilege he enjoyed. He had never been a sociable sort but now found himself on the edges of Margaret's wide set of connections. She introduced him to people all walks of life, including many of the musicians, conductors and legal professionals he otherwise encountered criminal proceedings. Margaret spoke to people with ease and grace. She asked about people's work, their family and had a remarkable ability for remembering the smallest of details – including names of their children and grandchildren. She managed to chat to the staff without condescending and asked questions without appearing intrusive. In short he was in awe of her personal skills and the ease with which she carried her social status.

This evening she wore a blue gown and a white angora wrap looking regal and yet unadorned by any jewellery. As they approached the large doors of the Ulster Hall she greeted Sir John and Lady Cressida Colliers. He noticed how warmly the two women spoke to each other and the cautious manner in which Sir John returned the greeting. Adams was a policeman at all times, even when off duty. Sir John was supercilious with the cloakroom staff but most attentive to those he saw as important.

As Margaret took her seat, some rows behind the Colliers she whispered to Adams. "John is always like that Bill. Don't give it another thought. He assumes that people are not aware of his ambitions to be national governor of the BBC – and therefore is prone to ingratiating himself to people he thinks will help him achieve that."

Policing experience of three decades told Bill Adams otherwise but he did not comment.

At the interval Colliers attempted to look unobtrusive as he networked the elite in the foyer. As he collected drinks for himself and Margaret Bill Adams heard him briefly chat with someone called Frederick Stewart – the same man who had made such a show of greeting Margaret when they had arrived. Margaret had been polite but rather cold in response.

Despite these thoughts the policeman found himself transported by the melodious harmonies of Chopin and the delightful company of dear Margaret.

When the recital came to a close rapturous applause filled the hall and the audience rose as one in approval. As the assembled throng dispersed, talking enthusiastically, Bill Adams wrestled with the desire to declare his undying love for Margaret. Instead he thanked her for a wonderful evening.

"Then we should do this again, Bill. I had no idea that you were such a music devotee."

Disappointed that she had not directly returned the compliment he straightened his shoulders and blurted out, "It is your company that is so marvellous Margaret. I would stand in the pouring rain just to be with you!" He blushed to the roots of his hair at his own words.

Margaret Beightin was as kind to him as she was dignified. "Bill Adams, I believe you have a crush on me! That is a lovely thing to say." She took his hand and squeezed it warmly. "Now let's get something to eat."

She convinced him that his adoration had gone unnoticed before but understood she must make up her mind about how she felt about him – that was only fair.

* * * * *

Nico sat under an angle-poise lamp in Eliza Taunter's office as he still thought of the room. Having seen his grandparents safely back to Marianne's he started into a four hour session of preparation for his teaching and supervision. Although quite confident that he was capable of these assignments, Nicola Tebaldi worked scrupulously to ensure he missed no detail. His task was made easier as he had access to Eliza's computer – staff passwords were regulated by security and he was given a new personal identity number alongside his contract and the keys to the office.

The professor's teaching materials were tidily filed by module and week number in Powerpoint presentations. He set about checking the detail of every slide only to find a number of citations were wrongly attributed – leaving the hallmark of plagiarism from websites. Finding how unreliable the late professor had been he selected what he would need for his teaching in the coming week and took quotations and references from his own work. It was simpler to start from scratch than to tinker with Eliza's work.

Her supervision commitments were filed separately, showing little understanding of the doctoral research of the five unfortunate postgraduate students who had fallen under her wing. The most honest thing to do was to read what each one had so far written up, meet with them and agree a way forward. He'd have to be tactful but he suspected he would encounter very grateful five postgrads – without recourse to comment on the late professor.

In truth he had never suspected Eliza was quite such a fraud. He was more surprised than angry although he took teaching and supervision as seriously as his own research and publication.

It was nearly three in the morning before he got to bed, weary but contented with his work and overjoyed to see his grandparents happily ensconced in Belfast – if only for a temporary visit. He fell asleep with warm memories of sitting in the farmhouse kitchen as a boy with Olivia cooking dinner and Mario reading him tales of daring deeds.

* * * * *

Veronica arranged to meet Mario and Olivia Tebaldi that afternoon. Marianne served home-made cakes and coffee for them in the kitchen.

Nico was present as translator, knowing his grandparents spoke a Veronese dialect in part – and that her teach-yourself-Italian was unlikely to stretch that far.

Mario and Olivia greeted Veronica with such great warmth and gratitude that she was taken aback. She pointed out that no-one could have ignored Nico's plight, adding that a younger and more athletic woman would not have twisted her ankle in process.

"You saved our precious Nico. He is our only grandson and we are forever in your debt, Veronica." Mario spoke with deep-seated emotion. Olivia nodded in agreement.

"Actually, I am a very nosey person and it my curiosity got the better of me. And it was Jack Summers who got into the house."

"Then we are also forever in his debt, dear lady." Olivia spoke for them both. "As we are here for such a short visit we would like to spend some of the time repaying your goodness. Would you and the Jack Summers man be free to have dinner with us this evening?"

Nico added, "It will be in Alberto's and I know you both appreciate his food!"

"How could I resist that? I would be delighted! Jack will be too, assuming he is free." Veronica relished the thought.

"Oh, he is free, Veronica. I asked him this morning and he will be there."

"Good, I know his Italian is much better than mine – you won't need Nico to translate everything.

* * * * *

Cressida Colliers booked the pre-Christmas river cruise on the dates she and Margaret had agreed. She opened her gardening diary and carefully penned in the dates and times of travel. Wistfully she looked through her study window into the carefully manicured garden, wondering how she would fill her days until then.

Downstairs a crashing noise and the sound of breaking glass brought her back to the present moment. She dropped her diary and went to see what had happened. As she reached the turn in the stairs she discovered Scarlet Woods, the housekeeper, lying bleeding on top of an antique mirror now smashed to smithereens.

"Scarlet!" Cressida shouted out but got no response. "John, come quickly there's been an awful accident!"

Colliers appeared from upstairs. The front hallway sparkled with shards of crystal glass in the middle of which lay a body, face down in a pool of blood that was spreading across he parquet floor.

"Don't touch a thing Cressida! Call an ambulance immediately and I will see if she is still alive." He gingerly stepped towards the body, trying to avoid getting blood on is shoes and put a finger to the carotid artery. There was no pulse.

When the ambulance arrived Scarlet Woods was pronounced dead. "The cause of death was almost certainly a shard of glass through the oesophagus."

Despite every appearance of a sorry accident the police were obliged to attend the scene. Since neither Sir John nor Lady Cressida had seen what had occurred they could only report the sounds they had heard. The presence of a small stepping stool overturned nearby made it reasonable to assume that the housekeeper had slipped and somehow brought the heavy antique looking glass down with her.

Cressida was shocked and seriously disturbed by the sight and was sitting in the drawing room sipping hot sugary tea with a policewoman at her side. Once he had given his statement Colliers excused himself and hoping to keep as far away as possible from witnessing his wife's distress.

"I must call my daughter. She will be able to look after her mother." He said by way of an excuse to absent himself.

"Indeed, Sir John that would probably be helpful." The policewoman hoped that the daughter was a more compassionate person than her father.

Colliers left the drawing room and proceeded towards the privacy of his own room. He rarely went into his wife's study, preferring to avoid her company and chattering other than at meal times. Perhaps it was instinct or just his fastidious reaction to seeing Cressida's diary lying untidily spread out on the floor. Whatever the motivation he went in rather than simply closing the door. The diary was open on the page where Cressida had made notes on Lebrocquy, Luke and Conor – plus the names Leo Richards and Peter Saunders. He suddenly felt exposed and angry. What was she doing interfering in his business? And why was she making detailed notes? She must be that informing Margaret Beightin woman!

Cold, calculating determination filled his mind. He would deal with that busybody of a wife once things had calmed down.

* * * * *

The table at Alberto's was cheerful. Mario, Olivia and Nico Tebaldi sat on one side facing Jack Summers and Veronica. As they made their way through a large platter of antipasti they chatted easily. Olivia was asking Jack about the rescue of Caro Nico. An astute woman she did not accept any story at face value.

"How did you get into the house?"

Before answering Jack looked at Veronica, as if to caution her not to be too specific. Olivia noticed and laughed. "Oh, so you were mischievous, then?"

Jack pursed his lips, put his index finger to them, nodded and winked at her.

"I won't ask more" She opened a new topic of conversation. "Nico tells me you know Tuscany well."

"Yes. When I was there recently I met a man you would know." He smiled. "Giacomo Dilucca."

Mario's eyes widened. "Dilucca the policeman?"

"Yes." Jack nodded. "He helped me organise Dad's funeral arrangements." He used the term without thinking, feeling a stab of grief.

"Yes, of course, my condolences Jack." Mario spoke softly.

"Thank you. I haven't talked about it much but I miss him terribly." Jack lower lip wobbled.

"Ah, we Italian men are much more emotional than you British and Irish." Mario was unsure about which nationality Jack would claim. "The bond of father and son is strong – I miss Nico's father terribly, even after all these years." There were tears in Mario's eyes.

"And yet we have Nico!" Olivia interrupted. "And we have to thank you and Veronica for saving him from that dungeon!" She lifted her glass and toasted "To the two redeeming rescuers!"

Nico and Mario raised their glasses. "To the two redeeming rescuers!"

Jack blushed and Veronica pursed her lips.

"I think you have thanked us quite enough. I am still more than curious about why Leo Richards imprisoned Nico in the first place – and cannot understand how the police believe he has simply vanished."

Jack said nothing but recalled his conversation with Giacomo Dilucca, and the suggestion that Richards was there in secret and up to some nefarious deed. He laughed. "You had better be careful. Veronica is a detective in her spare time! The next thing you know she will have you ensnared in her investigations." Although Jack did not use the word amateur Veronica wondered if had used the usual 'amateur sleuth' and as she did not grasp all his Italian she shot a warning glance at him.

Seeing this Nico intervened. "It is a compliment Veronica."

She relaxed and sipped her wine contentedly.

* * * * *

Secretary of State Clive Heedon sat in his well-appointed office flicking through papers on his large rosewood desk. He enjoyed what work he did and the Northern Ireland Civil Servants. They were much more compliant than their English counterparts, rarely displaying the sort of independence that Ministers in England had to endure. Permanent Secretaries had run the place for decades when the country was under the regime of Direct Rule from Westminster but less senior staff had not dared to question let alone challenge Ministers. Somehow that practice had remained delightfully unaltered.

When and if he asked advice he relied on the fact that he would usually be told what he wanted to hear. In particular he liked the do-nothing response to any controversy. Currently the hullabaloo was about flying flags – allegedly this had some effect on public order but this Secretary of State found the whole matter petty and unfathomable. What was the problem? Could the police not sort it out? It seemed tiresome and not something he'd expect in London.

He laughed remembering the day he had overheard an Assistant Secretary asking a subordinate about a letter. Pointing to the words pencilled in the margin 'spherical objects' he'd asked. "Who is spherical and to what does he object?"

The subordinate had coughed and replied that it was a mischievous critical comment. "Someone trying to be witty Sir."

He had changed the person assigned as his personal public servant after the embarrassment with those damned fake pictures. Of course the woman had been correct to warn him about the Beechlands Gallery but he had been stung for a large sum of money and although it was reimbursed he felt a certain awkwardness bordering on humiliation. A pleasant young man called Chris Barker was now his daily helper. It galled him that word might spread but he ignored that possibility and was happy that the subject was never spoken of again.

He thought about how practical and effective Sir John Colliers had been in the whole sorry business and wondered if he could help Colliers get the governorship at the BBC. Clive Heedon wielded considerable influence and felt he owed it to Colliers to back him. As he was due to see the man in the next few days he would seek out some information about the BBC post beforehand.

Calculating that Colliers would then be in his debt Clive Heedon was happy that the proper balance of things would then be restored. He lifted his phone and asked Chris Barker to get him a briefing on the National Governorship of BBC Northern Ireland.

Barker came into his office with a small folder and afternoon tea on a tray some fifteen minutes later.

* * * * *

Chapter Six

Jack Summers had been a policeman for almost his entire working life. His letter of resignation was carefully written and he reread it before putting it into an envelope and sealing it. He had left it for twenty four hours before lifting it from the mantelpiece and putting it into his pocket. It was bound for DCI Bill Adams' desk that morning.

He knew it was irrational but his encounter with Mario Tebaldi had broken through the protective shell that held back almost a lifetime of grief for his mother and lately the intense pain at the loss of his father. The old man's open emotion and compassion had gently penetrated the armour shield that encrusted him. Having experienced the poignancy of memory when he referred to his father as Dad, Jack felt a warm sense of acceptance slowly seeping into his whole being. He slept well that night and woke up refreshed, alert and happily settled.

He was not at all sure what he was going to do when he left his job but decided he would just give it time. After a long hot shower and a light breakfast he was positively cheerful. He strode into Donaghdubh station with energy and purpose.

* * * * *

Margaret had asked Veronica to her home for coffee. She wanted to make it crystal clear that the cottage was Veronica's place and she would only appear when invited. Although reluctant to discuss her relationship with Bill Adams Lady Margaret Beightin found Veronica a trustworthy confidant – and discretion was essential.

While a holiday romance was hardly a scandal Margaret kept her own counsel on all matters of the heart concerning herself. The situation with Bill Adams was different. For one thing Veronica knew him – although she suspected Bill's unfavourable opinion Veronica's was fully reciprocated.

However, the priority for their chat was the obscurity of the source of the paintings in the Stewart Gallery.

"How lovely, Veronica. It's just like old times!" Margaret greeted her friend warmly. "I take it everything is as it should be at the cottage?"

"It is Margaret but I am renting a place in Belfast. Living in a single room is best left as a short-lived pleasure. I have taken a garden flat on a short lease." Veronica would have bitten out her tongue before admitting she had felt bullied and resentful towards Margaret. "So thank you so much but I shan't be taking the cottage."

Margaret served coffee and they sat outside. Margaret showed no obvious sign of disappointment but disliked her friend's ingratitude. Veronica did not smoke, although she wanted to. Leaving aside her frustration with Veronica and her preoccupation with Bill Adams Margaret started by outlining her suspicions about the paintings Frederick Stewart was selling.

"I am not at all sure where they came from or if I am seeing too much into things but my instinct tells me there is some fraud and my knowledge of Luke tells me that painting is a counterfeit." She paused and nibbled at the fairy cake on her plate. "I do think the Lebrocquy is genuine, however."

"You were very impressive, Lady Beightin, at the viewing. You could have kept him going for hours – of course I was running out of things to say." Veronica finished her coffee sensing Margaret's disapproval but determined to ignore that for the time being.

"Colliers is mixed up in all this. Cressida told me the names of the artists – and they are exactly the same as those we saw. I must contact her and see if there is anything else she can tell us."

"Us? What help do you think I can be?" Veronica was flabbergasted. "I am a total Philistine!"

"You are a first class detective, my dear. All we need is some more information and the authentication from the National Gallery and then we can look into the matter further."

"I don't suppose you could push Stewart a bit harder about who is selling these pictures?"

"I could try but he'd probably talk about privacy, discretion and client confidentiality – as if he were a doctor or a priest!" Margaret spat the words out, showing some frustration and an evident distaste for Frederick Stewart. "And these days you would be amazed at how many people need to sell their precious works of art."

"How are you going to get out of buying the Lebrocquy? You don't actually have that amount of money, do you?"

"Of course not, but his work is no longer attracting the same amounts. Last year the price dropped by more than a third." She paused, only now thinking about how she'd extricate herself from what Stewart believed was a certain deal. "I will just have to confess that I do not have such money, that I was captivated by it but cannot actually afford it." She gave a feigned prissy smile prompting Veronica to laugh out loud – but warily, having been on the receiving end of her anger.

"Margaret you should have been on the stage!"

"Speaking of stages I was at a Chopin recital with Bill Adams last night." She glanced to see Veronica's reaction. Since there was not the customary grimace that came with mention of DCI Adams she continued. "He announced a profound affection for me – the poor man was so flustered I held his hand to comfort him."

Stifling the urge to say she was surprised to hear Adams could harbour such sentiments for anyone Veronica pursed her lips. "That's a very delicate situation. I think you were very kind to him. Now do you like him? Do you like him enough to take it further?" She was searching for a more demure turn of phrase than the words that immediately sprang to mind.

"He is a nice man and I do enjoy his company." She looked at her friend.

"Well, tell him that. Tell him you enjoy his company and would like to see him. If things take a turn for the romantic so be it, but for the moment you feel companionship is enough. How does that sound?"

"How gracefully you put it. Thank you Veronica. I think that is a good approach. At this stage of my life I don't expect long term romantic relationships."

They both knew this did not solve the dilemma but that it was a credible and careful ploy for the immediate future.

* * * * *

Nico organised a viewing of seven Montague Road for the afternoon. Eager to please and anxious to get a sale Mr Sells was early. Nico saw him from next door.

"Nonno, the estate agent is here. He is early but shall we go now?"

"I think he can wait Nico. We will go as arranged." He smiled benevolently at his grandson. "You don't want him to think you are so interested."

"Oh, I have not shown any enthusiasm. I remember how you have always made transactions and maybe I was too cool. Still you are right we will go in ten minutes."

Nico appeared at the open door of number seven with Mario and Olivia and introduced them to Mr Sells.

"These are my grandparents Mr Sells, Mario and Olivia Tebaldi." As the estate agent held out his hand in greeting, Nico added. "They are keen to see the house but they do not speak more than a little English."

Handshakes were formally exchanged. Mario nodded and smiled at Mr Sells. Olivia eyed the man with obvious suspicion. Nico restrained himself as he watched the pair enacting the same ritual he had seen in the markets around Poggiduomo many times. They were a great double act.

Where Mario looked at the structural features Olivia looked at the light and space carefully calculating how much work would be entailed in making the place habitable. Keith Sells cringed as Mario used a butter knife from Marianne's kitchen to test for rot in wooden window frames and skirting boards – but he said nothing.

Olivia inspected what furniture had not been disposed of without showing any sign of approval. Nico had decided that he would buy the house if he could negotiate a price he could afford. He kept an eye on Sells who was nervously assessing Mario and Olivia – as he was certain they would be making the decision, and probably bankrolling the deposit. He was so wrong.

In less than forty minutes Mario and Olivia had seen all they needed, and announced that they were finished.

"Thank you Mr Sells. I appreciate you accommodating my grandparents. As I am their only grandchild they are concerned about how I make such a large decision."

"Sells and Company has a mission statement Doctor Tebaldi – nothing is too much trouble for a client. I am happy that you wanted a second viewing."

Olivia shook her head, making Sells anxious once again.

"I shall discuss it with my grandparents and get back to you. Have you any other interested parties at the moment?" Nico imagined he could smell the salesman's fear.

"No, not just at the moment. In fact that may be to your benefit Doctor Tebaldi!" He tried to sound enthusiastic.

"Then, I shall come back to you by the end of tomorrow Mr Sells."

They parted company and the three Tebaldis returned to the sunroom in number five to go over the details.

Mario and Olivia were expressionless until they had closed the front door of Marianne's house. Then they both laughed aloud. Mario hugged his grandson. "You have learned a lot more than just bookish things my dear Nico!"

"You would do well in any market!" Olivia added. "That man thinks we are going to buy the house – he was very anxious to please us!"

"So you think it is a sound proposition?"

"It does not seem like the scene of such dreadful crimes and it is a fine house." Olivia pronounced.

"Indeed, if the price is good it would be a fine investment." Mario declared.

Nico was content with that. He would broach the subject of their coming to live with him after a deal had been sealed.

* * * * *

Despite Cressida Colliers' best efforts to conceal the bruising on her neck under make-up it was apparent. Her face somehow hollowed out. Margaret was horrified when she caught sight of her in the Merchant Bistro. She approached the table hastily setting her coat on a chair and sitting down.

"Cressida! What on earth has happened to you?" She whispered in horror.

"Scarlet had a fatal accident yesterday – killed by falling onto the mirror in our hall – it was broken in the fall." Her voice was shaky and her hands trembling.

"Were you caught up in the fall?" Margaret asked.

"No, I found her lying in a pool of blood. John felt for a pulse but there was none."

"In that case, why have you got bruising on your neck?" Margaret was concerned because she immediately suspected Colliers had injured his wife.

"Oh Margaret I am so ashamed!" There were tears in Cressida's eyes. "John was so very angry with me." She sobbed quietly into a handkerchief.

"He did this?" Margaret could not hide her outrage. "What made him angry?" She felt a strong indignation course through her veins, and clenched her fists tightly.

"He found my gardening diary – I dropped it when I heard the crash and went downstairs to see what had happened. I had made a note of the painters I told you about."

"Why would that annoy him? You only gave me three names." Margaret was genuinely at a loss as to why the names of these artists would induce such fury in Colliers.

"Is that all I told you? It was my notes about the men with whom he dealt that seemed to enrage him. He said I was interfering with his business – and grilled me about whether I had talked to anyone about it."

"And he hit you?" Margaret spat out the words.

"Several times but after the first blow I felt no fear." Cressida's hands had stopped shaking and her voice was steady. "I have decided to leave him – though he doesn't know that yet."

"Good for you Cressida. The man is a brute! And my door is always open – if you want to come to me at any time – day or night." Margaret's wrath was now replaced with compassion and delight that Cressida was not going to stay in her dreadful marriage.

"I now think there is something dubious about his business as he calls it. There must be something he wants desperately to hide." Her voice resonated with a desire to hit back at him,

"So what exactly did you write down? Can you remember in detail?" Margaret would willingly collude in a vendetta against this degenerate wife-beater!

"Not a lot – and John ripped out the pages and burned them. I listed the artists which I told you about and the names of the two men who negotiated and delivered the paintings."

"Aha! Then their names must be significant. What were they?"

"Leo Richards and Peter Saunders. The first negotiated the sale and the price and provided the documentation. The second man delivered the paintings."

"Do you remember when he took possession of these paintings, by any chance?"

"It was at the end of September – the last Tuesday." She sounded certain. "He was like a child in a sweet shop – so pleased with himself."

"How did you get that information?"

"It was a comment you made about Lebrocquy – though I believe you thought it went over my head." As Margaret blushed in shame Cressida continued. "I asked him to humour me and tell me what had made him so happy. He gave me a lecture about the artists and I didn't even have to ask for the names – he got carried away with his own patter."

Margaret laughed out loud. "Cressida – my apologies for seeming to condescend – and my congratulations on your intelligent sleuthing!"

"Now I could do with some strong coffee!" Cressida spoke in a light hearted but determined tone.

* * * * *

George Summers had left money for his young friend and house-sitter Nico. With that and his prudent savings there was enough for a modest deposit on seven Montague Road. Good fortune had given him professional promotion and assured his finances for the immediate future. What Nico had not taken into account was the longer term – that was a risk that he now simply had to take.

Mario and Olivia did not take the return flight to Verona. Mario had a heart attack and was rushed to hospital the morning before they were due to depart.

Nico was supposed to be taking his first supervision session with a second year doctoral student but was needed as translator in the emergency room where Olivia was distressed and unable to tell the medical team what they needed to know. He texted the young man offering profound apologies and explaining his absence, with a promise to make up for this dereliction of duty. He added a few comments on student's research and current write-up – which were complimentary on balance but critical of the direction in which Professor Taunter had been pushing his work.

In the taxi on the way to the hospital he got a response. "Nico. No probs. Can rearrange. We all know u will do a fine job. Thanx for compliments. So glad to have a new supervisor. If it helps my father is a consultant cardiologist here. Say hello for me. Jim Andrews."

Mr Andrews was expecting Nico – Jim had texted him. "Ah you must be the famous Nico. We have stabilised your grandfather you can see him later when we get him into a bed. Your grandmother is very distressed so perhaps you could explain that he is not going to die and we can probably get him into shape with medication. There is a café on the first floor where you can get coffee and I will ensure you are both brought up to see Mr Tebaldi as soon as possible."

"Thank you Mr Andrews. I will go to her now. And my apologies for missing Jim's supervision session."

"I happen to know that he is overjoyed to have you as a supervisor – your reputation precedes you Doctor Tebaldi!" Jeff Andrews offered his hand and Nico shook it with gratitude and relief.

Olivia was distressed in a way that emergency staff recognise. She was white, silent and stared in fear. She was not weeping.

"Nonna! The consultant says Nonno is going to be okay – he isn't going to die. Let's go and get some coffee and I will explain what is happening. Now take my arm." He spoke softly, gently and with great care.

He spent the rest of the morning with his grandmother and they spoke to Mario at midday.

"You gave us a scare Nonno but the doctor assures me that you will recover." Nico stood beside his grandmother who was seated holding Mario's hand and gently stroking it.

"Oh Mario!" She sobbed at the sight of her man who God had granted deliverance.

"Carissima. Calm yourself." Mario whispered to reassure her. "I will be out of here soon. Now you go back with Nico and I will sleep until this evening. You can come back then."

Olivia blew her nose and straightened the scarf around her neck. She breathed in and rose steadily to her feet. She gave Mario a big grin and said "Now you behave with all these beautiful nurses, my old man!"

"I will. Now Nico you finish that business." His voice was hoarse but still quite strong.

Olivia left the ward having composed herself and regained what she thought of as the correct dignity for an Italian in a foreign country. Nico felt his heart would burst with the strength of emotion – he was so grateful for the way things had turned out.

He accompanied Olivia back to Marianne's, impatient to ensure that she could stay there for the time being. He also felt it was time to introduce the idea of them coming to live in Belfast with him. That would have to wait until they were together – even if that had to be in a hospital.

As he had promised Nico contacted Mr Sells, explaining that his grandfather had just had a heart attack and that he wanted to make an agreement – as long as the price was right. Sells sensed the immediacy. "I am at your disposal Doctor Tebaldi – at whatever time suits you."

Nico had his grandfather in mind when he entered the offices of Sells and Company. He would drive a hard bargain – in the hope of reserving some of his accrued monies to start work on the house immediately. He succeeded in that objective leaving Mr Sells feeling content to forgo some commission in order to get that unspeakable place off his books.

* * * * *

DCI Bill Adams was reluctant to accept Jack Summers' letter of resignation at face value and said so. "Jack are you sure about this? I mean you have just had a bereavement and I don't think this is the best time to be making such significant decisions." He sighed. "You are a good detective – too good to just walk away from almost a lifetime of police work. Would you take some compassionate leave and keep your letter until you have had more time to think about it?"

"I'd prefer to leave the letter with you, Sir, but I will take some leave." He did not say that he was sure about resigning and his father's death had simply precipitated a decision that he'd have come to anyway. "I'm not up to the job at the moment – though Gary McClure would cover for me. If I may I'll get back to you in a fortnight."

"Fine, Jack. I do hope you will reconsider." Adams nodded and clenched his jaw.

Jack left Donaghdubh police station with a sense of closure and the beginnings of elation. He had always suspected his father would have preferred him to have followed another career and he was now going to do that. He looked up into the clear blue sky, certain there was no heaven up there but psychologically addressing his father. Jack was going to take another direction as of now.

* * * * *

Mario Tebaldi made as good a recovery as possible and, duly medicated was discharged from hospital in a few days. He had spent some of that time considering Nico's suggestion that he and Olivia come to live with him in Belfast – in the house he had bought. He returned to number five Montague Road and a much happier Olivia.

As this was the first occasion that he had enough time to discuss the proposal in detail with his wife he settled into an armchair in their room and began.

"Olivia my dearest, what do you think? This is a foreign country and we speak so little English."

"You are still here to speak, thank God! I thought I was going to lose you Mario." Her voice was firm but warm. "Here we have Nico and could learn enough English to get by. In Italy we will be alone." A practical countrywoman and in better health than her husband she had accepted that she might well be literally alone in Italy in time to come. The idea of living with Nico made this a much less frightening prospect.

Sensing that his wife had just such an eventuality in mind Mario spoke. "This time I was lucky and the hospital here is very good – better than at home – but I won't live for ever, Olivia. I would like you to have Nico to look after you. Of course we should make sure that Nico did not make the offer because I was in hospital."

"Yes he is young and when he gets a wife she may not want us in her home. We must remind him of that."

"Perhaps you can wash dishes at Alberto's!" He teased his wife.

Nico would put their minds at rest. He wanted to have them near him if they could bear to leave their homeland.

"We are leaving the only home we have ever had – to move to an apartment, Nico." Mario reassured him. "However, if we do come to your home you must accept money from the sale of the farm. We have our pride!" Mario was embarrassed at the speed with which he had accepted his grandson's offer – old age and heart problems made him sentimental and sensitive.

"Of course Nonno!" Nico suddenly feared that pride might be a real obstacle to his plans. "Still, you must remember that I owe you and Nonna so much. You have given me a home and an education." He spoke with great emotion.

"Your grandfather will set the sale of the farm in motion. He knows a developer who wants our land." Olivia asserted so that the conversation came to an end.

* * * * *

Margaret Beightin had written down the names of the men Colliers had been dealing with and was now impatient to hear news of the authentication of the Lebrocquy painting. She had no excuse for going to the Stewart Gallery until that had been obtained. In the meantime she kept in constant touch with Cressida.

As a longstanding friend Margaret was reluctant to share Cressida's confidences, even with Veronica. Instead they discussed the mystery of the missing Nicola Tebaldi and the murdered Eliza Taunter.

"I find it hard to believe that there is nothing linking the two events." Veronica was frustrated that no leads had been found. "Both crimes were committed in the same house. Obviously the murder is much more serious but Nico could have starved to death in that dungeon of a basement."

"And you say that he is buying the house? I find that most peculiar. Anyone else would never want to step into that place again!"

"Indeed, I still think it's a bit creepy. The police could not trace Eliza's ex-husband." Veronica wondered how Leo Richards had just disappeared into thin air. "No-one knows why he was here since he lives in Manchester. Oh where are you, Leo Richards?"

"Did you say Leo Richards? I've heard that name before!" Margaret was startled but also cautious and a dutiful friend. Could she mention what she knew without betraying Cressida's undisclosed secret?

"Where and in what connection?" Veronica lit on this fact. It was a tiny spark of light in the darkness of the mystery. "Leo Richards was the man who abducted Nico!"

"Really?" Margaret was shocked. "But he was the man who negotiated the sale of paintings with that pig Colliers!" She could not disguise her noticeable hatred of the man.

"What? He was in Eliza's house and shut Nico into the basement." Veronica Pilchard was thinking, computing every detail she could recall. "Perhaps he was the stranger I saw coming out of Eliza's with a bundle – after the murder!"

"What bundle?" Margaret shook her head. "No, Veronica it could not have been Leo Richards. He was not the man who actually delivered the paintings. The man who brought them to Colliers was Peter Saunders."

"That seems an odd arrangement I mean to deal with one person and then have another do the delivery. It's not as if these are photographs or books. Why would Leo Richards entrust a real Lebrocquy – about which, by the way, I am quite certain – to someone else?"

"I have no idea. All I know is that Richards did the negotiation, providing the documentation and Saunders did the delivery."

"And as we know Leo Richards has disappeared." Veronica rubbed her chin in thought. "Okay, we know the names of the two involved in the art deal. We know that Richards was Nico's kidnapper. There just has to be a link between the art deal and Eliza Taunter's house."

"Veronica, if the police cannot trace Leo Richards do you think they could trace Peter Saunders?"

"Of course! As ever, my dear Lady Beightin, you have got to the nub of the issue. Surely Saunders cannot have disappeared as well?" Had it been anyone other than Margaret she would have slapped her on the back. "Good thinking!" Veronica's recent umbrage against Margaret evaporated in her enthusiasm for investigating.

"Now all we have to do is get the police to find Peter Saunders."

Veronica was now less than wholehearted about keeping her promise to DI Emily Brown. She had offered to come back with any recollection or information that might help but she had the bit between her teeth – Veronica Pilchard was in full sleuthing mode.

* * * * *

Cressida consulted a solicitor who'd advised her to get medical evidence confirming the gravity of the beating Colliers had inflicted on her. Armed with this she returned to Jessica Joyce and asked that divorce proceeding be put on hold until she had left the family home.

"I do not wish to have any dramatics so I will find somewhere first and then come back to you." Cressida sighed. "I understand that you know my husband's solicitor but I rely on your professional confidence."

"Lady Colliers, wild horses could not drag a single word out of me!" Jessica Joyce declared. "I deal with a lot of cases in which the partner has been at fault – and with one exception over the past twenty years the husband is the violent one. I should tell you that I detest both the offenders and their counsel. I would never do business with their legal advisers!" She smiled reassuringly at Cressida.

"Please, call me Cressida. And thank you, Jessica. This is new territory for me." Cressida was growing slightly more confident as the consultation continued.

"Its territory that will take you to a much better place Cressida." The solicitor said with conviction and the certainty of long practice. "You will need to put some thought into the settlement – and take a strong negotiating position from the start. We can back down if needs be, but I advise my clients to go in prepared to be ruthless – sadly that is the way these cases go."

"I am rather nervous about creating any unnecessary animosity, to be honest." Although she was determined to get the legal separation she knew her husband was a very sore loser and would be furious at the social consequences of divorce. Her face expressed that fear – very clearly.

"By the expression on your face I take that you anticipate antagonism, Cressida?" Jessica Joyce had seen that haunted look too many times to misinterpret its source. "That is what I am here to do – I have the task of being objective, making your case and protecting you and your interests." Seeing that she was not convincing her intimidated client she continued. "I have known cases where the husband has tried to have his wife certified as insane."

Cressida flinched. That was precisely the sort of action that she expected from Colliers. She had seen his attempts at ruining the reputation of social rivals – but she could be sure he would be more ferocious than that towards her.

"So he is, in fact, a nasty piece of work?" Jessica pouted and shrugged. "That will make my job a good deal easier. Vindictive partners, male or female, lose the judge's sympathy fairly quickly. I will draw out the poison and anger in him – have no fear! I realise that this is completely new ground for you but I have been in practice for so long that I know every turn of the game. And be assured when the legal people start it is a game but one that I have never lost in cases such as yours."

Jessica Joyce could see that Cressida had taken enough on board and suggested that they talk again before serving any papers. She made it clear that if she had concerns or wanted to defer – or even change her mind – that Cressida was calling the shots. "I am here do take your instructions – to use the formal language – so remember that. You tell me what you want and I follow orders." She gave Cressida her card – writing her personal phone number on the back.

"If you are worried about anything just give me a call, even out of office hours."

* * * * *

The residents of Wild Fern Alley gathered for an autumn clear-up, under the guidance of the bird woman as they called the ornithologist. Seed heads and scrub was to be left in large part to encourage insects – and hedgehogs if they were very lucky – and provide winter forage for the birds.

Not everyone was as devoted to the survival of the swift population as the bird woman. The work put in over the past six months had resulted in an accumulation of tub, pots and containers bursting with annual flowers, shrubs, young fruit trees and herbs as well as ferns. The hanging baskets now past their best and in need of renewal.

Adam and Steve were eager to comply – although not keen on the increasing numbers of squirrels. Desmond said nothing but his pursed lips expressed a certain scepticism – he like things to be tidy.

Marianne asked for assurances that these measures would not encourage rodents. The elderly Mrs Wilson offered to put out bird food.

Underlying concerns, however, were about the possibility that rodents in the form of property magnates would reappear.

* * * * *

Veronica Pilchard was full of energy and sleeping well in her new flat in Mrs Wilson's home. She was spending a lot of her time producing investigative features for the Barry Doyle show – and some snatched hours with Mitchell. However, she was still engrossed by the mysterious events in seven Montague Road.

Central to her preoccupation was the question of how to trace Peter Saunders. Could she push Jack Summers into helping her? Veronica should, of course, have gone back to DCI Emily Brown but she had a strong sense that she could solve these crimes without further official help.

She called Jack on the off-chance that he was available for a chat and was delighted to discover he was on leave. She did not ask why. She was too selfish to do that. "Jack, I need some advice. How do you go about tracing someone? Can you check air travel?"

Jack sighed. "Veronica Pilchard you are back sleuthing again!" He laughed, which took her by surprise. "Come over for a coffee and tell me what you know – or should I say suspect."

This was not the Jack Summers she had known before. He would have cautioned her severely. Veronica determined to take full advantage of the change – even if it was to be short-lived. "I'm in town now. I could be with you in half an hour."

"Now, Veronica, you will have to be completely honest with me if you expect any help!" His tone was sharp. Perhaps he was not so changed as she'd thought.

* * * * *

Wild Fern Alley was ablaze with autumnal colour. Desmond Charles was on his knees weeding out thistles – surreptitiously as it had been agreed that seeds should be left for the declining population of swifts. He preferred to keep the patch behind his house tidy. As it was early morning he was not expecting any company and therefore jumped when he heard the lock of a yard door being opened. He looked around to see Nico at the far end of the alley. He waved and pushed the trough of weeds behind him.

"Good morning Desmond!" A smiling Nico approached.

"Good Morning Nico." Desmond's face reddened.

Nico approached still smiling, wholly ignorant of the collective agreements made about Wild Fern Alley "How diligent you are – and so early!"

"Actually Nico, we are supposed to leave all the weeds for birds but I can't bear the mess. I'd be grateful if you didn't mention this." Desmond was visibly embarrassed.

"Why of course not!" Nico nodded to seal their complicity. "As I am to be a permanent neighbour I would not dream of it."

"Please tell me all your news." Desmond smiled and relaxed but was unable to contain his curiosity.

"I have bought seven Montague Road and my grandparents are going to come and live with me."

"After all that has happened there? Are you not superstitious about the murder – and your own experience there?"

"That has worked to my advantage. I negotiated a very good price." Nico saw Desmond's face crease in disbelief. "In Poggiduomo where I grew up with my grandparents there are many houses with such gruesome history. After the war there were many grisly murders – as we Italians changed sides and fought each other. We take no notice – it is only bricks and mortar." He laughed. "Of course I didn't tell Mr Sells that!"

"I hear the place was in a ghastly state." Desmond was still curious and hoped to draw out the conversation. "It used to be a lovely place. My mother knew Mrs Stock the woman Eliza bought the house from."

"And is Mrs Stock still alive?"

"Oh yes! She is alive and well and moving out of the nursing home." Desmond's eyes narrowed. "I always thought Eliza bamboozled her – she wasn't all that confused. Eliza went to visit her a lot of times before she bought the house – and every time Mrs Stock seemed more confused and forgetful. I had my suspicions I can tell you." Desmond threw his hands up in the air in affectation.

"I would like to meet her because there are books and photographs that must be hers and I would like to return them." Nico looked into Desmond's face. "Do you know how I could contact her?"

"Yes. I will get you the number of the home. She is still there."

"Good. I will not be keeping these things but if there is a rightful owner I feel strongly I should return them."

Nico's kind-heartedness would bring him into contact with the woman who would unlock the secrets of seven Montague road.

* * * * *

Sir John Colliers was quite unaware of the fact that his wife was about to leave home and divorce him. Cressida Colliers had finally reached snapping point. She had tolerated his bullying and contempt for years. Now she was signing a short-term lease for a riverside apartment in South Belfast and unobtrusively moving personal possessions into Margaret's home. Fortunately Cressida did not depend on the meagre housekeeping that he put into her account each month. She had always been financially independent and now that she was taking steps towards personal independence her confidence increased slowly but noticeably. One of the first things she did was to visit Curl up and Dye and have her hair style changed.

"I do believe a subtle hint of colour would suit you very well Lady Colliers." Desmond suggested gently. "Here are a few pictures of the look I recommend. What do you think?"

"Are you sure that would be a touch young for me?" Cressida felt every year of her age.

"Not at all Lady Colliers! You have such good bone structure and the style you have at the moment doesn't do it justice." Desmond chatted away, ignoring the traces of bruising under cosmetics on her neck, and cursing his own gender. Why did some men have to be such brutes? He went on, "It's a classic style. My mother had something similar – and such fine features! As you can see I have not taken after her – nature was not that kind."

"Please call me Cressida." She was considering a future under her maiden name and therefore without the honorary title. "If you think so. You are the professional!" She smiled.

"I will work my magic and you will leave here feeling like a million dollars!" Desmond felt a stab of deep sympathy for the downtrodden woman. He would transform her appearance within a couple of hours.

As she prepared to pay and leave, feeling a boost of confidence far exceeding any rational explanation, Desmond disappeared into the staff room and reappeared with a sky blue silk scarf. It was his but he lied. "Cressida, if you will excuse me being so pass-remarkable, I think this would suit you a good deal more than that camel colour. This scarf has been here for positively eons and whoever left it has never come back for it. Would you?" He handed her the fine fabric scarf. As she put it around her neck he squealed. "My dear goodness – I had not noticed how very blue your eyes are! Lovely! Health to wear."

Unused to such complimentary attention Cressida shone with pleasure. She donned her coat, left with a confident gait and made her way to Margaret Beightin's home.

* * * * *

Jack Summers was his own man now. He was still formally a policeman but he knew he would not return to his post again. In the meantime Veronica Pilchard was urging him into what he knew would be risky ground.

"Who is it that you are so keen to trace – and why?" His tone was abrupt but not hostile.

"Peter Saunders. It's a long story but he and Leo Richards were the two men who did an art deal with Sir John Colliers which Margaret thinks is suspicious. Remember Leo Richards was the one who abducted Nico? He appears to have vanished from the surface of the earth. It was Saunders who handed over the paintings to Colliers and we estimate that he made the delivery around the time of Eliza Taunter's murder." She made the case succinctly hoping Jack's affection for the young Italian might add to its weight. "Unless Saunders lives here he must have travelled. How can I find out?"

"You can't and you must know that. What you mean is how can I find out?" He looked her straight in the eye, moved his head sideways and pursed his lips.

"Oh Jack, would you?" She pleaded without a trace of shame. "Can you do that?"

"You know you should take any information to Emily Brown. I should tell her." He watched her reaction.

"I suppose so." She dropped her head in disappointment. "I just wanted ..." Her voice trailed off.

"Just wanted to outsmart the cops. Veronica Pilchard you are incorrigible!" Jack chuckled quietly. "However, on this occasion I will indulge you. I can make a few calls."

Astonished that she had managed to persuade him Veronica squealed in delight. "Jack Summers you are such a star!"

"No, just feeling a bit reckless – and this goes no further. I can make enquiries off the record."

"Fine. I won't breathe a word – promise."

In less than two hours the travel arrangements and journeys taken by Peter Saunders in the last days of September were known to Jack Summers if not yet officially by the police. Inevitably, Jack knew, the matter would have to be dealt with by the proper authorities but it might be helpful if there was some evidence pointing towards the murderer if not also the creature who had imprisoned Nico.

* * * * *

Nico started his search for Mrs Stock as soon as he got the phone number. He arranged for her to come and claim anything that she wanted from her former home. Although he was not concerned that the house had been the scene of a violent murder he was superstitious about making a good start in the place where he was to bring his grandparents.

Mrs Stock was a tall woman in her later seventies or early eighties. She had a strong voice and a slight Antrim accent although she had been born in Belfast. Nico greeted her at the front door and ushered her inside. "It is strange to invite you to your own home but as I said I wish to make the proper start here. There are photographs and things that must be yours and which you should have."

"Thank you I am very grateful. When I left I was so confused that I only took a picture and my clothes." She looked around the industrially cleaned hallway. "Of course I heard about the murder. Dreadful business altogether!"

"Where would you like to start?" Nico said.

"In the basement. There is a hidden storage space there and I kept letters there and some jewellery."

Nico followed her as she stepped, sure footed, down into the basement. She stood by the window from which Nico had cried for help. It was now clean and light poured into the enclosed space. She reached up and pulled on a coat hook on the wall. A trap door rose from the flag stones on the floor opening into a chamber underneath.

Nico gasped in awe. "A secret cave!"

"Yes, Nico. It was built when our men were being hunted down by the police. It was a hiding place and no-one spoke about it." She shrugged. "Those days are over now but that was a bad time."

She looked puzzled. "Someone has been here. I can't remember if I told Eliza about this but you can see my letters have been disturbed." A heap of envelopes lay in the corner. Whatever jewellery had been there was now gone.

"Oh I am so sorry." Nico was angry that some thief had taken her treasure.

"That is not important now. I am old and they weren't worth much." Her voice was steady. "If you look you can see where something has been dragged over the dust."

Nico bent down and picked up the envelopes carefully placing them on the clean floor of the basement above their heads. "At least we can save these." At the bottom of the heap was a scrap of paper. It was not part of the consignment of old letters. It was the stub of a boarding pass with a flight number on it.

Thinking himself rather melodramatic, but still wondering if it might belong to Leo Richards he took out a paper handkerchief and carefully retrieved it.

Mrs Stock saw this and fumbled in her handbag. "Take a plastic bag."

"You don't miss a trick do you?" Nico laughed.

"I heard about your stay in the basement – I still get the gossip from Desmond Charles. He visits me you know."

"Then you will know more about what's going on than I!" Nico liked the woman and thought his grandmother might get along with her. "Now let's have a look at books and anything you want from the kitchen. I understand that you are going to move out of the nursing home so you will need some of your own things back."

"You are very considerate Nico. There are a few small things I could use but I never was much of a cook."

Mrs Stock did not want many things. She looked through the kitchen cupboards and drawers and took out some old china and cutlery.

"Is that all you want? I have several boxes for you to pack as much as you need."

"Oh this is quite enough. I will buy some new things." She opened at the last cupboard and took out an MP3 recorder. "This certainly isn't mine!"

"I must have been Eliza's." Nico noticed a small blood stain on the play/record button. He took the small machine and put it back, carefully but firmly closing the cupboard. "All very unpleasant."

Mrs Stock was not sure whether he was referring to Eliza or the murder and did not comment.

* * * * *

Wild Fern Alley won the City Flowers Award – being the only entrant in its category that had made such a dramatic transformation of three adjoining alleys. Their inclusion of bird-friendly measures and the partially restored old cobble stones added to its merit according to the three judges. Marianne and Thaddeus were informed by letter and invited to the award winning ceremony at City Hall, along with up to seven other members of their group.

The prestige of this event was an important political device for rising local representatives – and Councillor Cobbles in particular. His ambitions for the mayoral seat drove him to accept the invitation to present the trophy to Marianne Kelly.

Chapter Eight

Margaret was satisfied that her judgement had proven correct. The National Gallery authenticated the Lebrocquy painting as the genuine article. Unfortunately for Frederick Stewart the expert's eye had also fallen on the John Luke and William Conor paintings. These had all been deemed counterfeit.

As she reread the official communication she thought of Sir John Colliers. He would find his nemesis – both in the failed art deal and in upcoming divorce case. Should she tell Cressida? Certainly she would tell Veronica!

She texted a terse "Lebrocquy genuine. Others are fake!!" She snapped her phone shut with a smile that verged on malicious. Oh she hated that pig Colliers!

Within minutes she got a reply. "Must meet up and decide further action. V."

Margaret texted back, "Can u make afternoon tea at four?"

* * * * *

Veronica only knew Cressida Colliers from the pages of the Ulster Tattler and was therefore unsure if it was the same woman she met leaving Margaret's home as she arrived.

"I don't think you have met." Margaret smiled. "Veronica this is Cressida Colliers. Cressida this is Veronica Pilchard."

The two women shook hands and exchanged greetings. Instinct told Veronica not to mention Richards or Saunders – or engage Cressida in any small talk. Instead she remarked on her appearance. "I think the pictures I've seen of you in the Tattler don't do you justice."

"I've had a bit of a makeover, that's all." Cressida said with reserve but trying to look cheerful.

"And she has been to Curl up and Dye!" Margaret added.

"Desmond is one of the best. He never fails to work miracles on my hair – but he also manages to make me feel so much better and confident!" Veronica spoke with sincerity as she trusted Desmond more than nearly anyone – and now this included Margaret.

"Well I must be on my way. Good to meet you at last. Margaret has told me so much about you." Cressida had a social manner similar to Margaret's.

Veronica wondered if that was due to their common experiences in school or just a generational thing. "And you. I hope we will meet again."

Cressida lifted the last of her possessions into the boot of her car, nodded to Margaret and got into her Jaguar. She waved and drove away. Today she was taking ownership of her new life. She was moving into her flat and had Jessica Joyce start divorce proceedings. She had released herself from the bonds of a long and unhappy marriage. On the passenger seat a silver sugar bowl gleamed. It was her house warming present from Margaret and she treasured it as a token of her new-found freedom. Neither John nor Belinda knew where she was going.

"Your friend looks a good deal more relaxed and happy than the pictures of her that I have seen." Veronica could not resist prying.

"Now Veronica!" Margaret admonished. She was not about to reveal her friend's personal and as yet secret affairs.

"Sorry." Veronica said without a trace of regret. There was more to Lady Colliers than met the eye. "Now tell me your news."

"The paintings that Colliers bought and passed on the Frederick Stewart are as I suspected fake – with the exception of the Lebrocquy." Margaret Beightin asserted with vigour. "I wouldn't trust that gallery and I think that now is the time to take this further."

"How can you do that?" Veronica was genuinely bewildered.

"I think the Fraud Squad would be interested in these authentication documents from the National Gallery." She held out a sheaf of papers in a theatrical gesture – grinning widely. She had demanded that she receive copies at the same time as Frederick Stewart. "I think they will want to ask some very searching questions."

"Oh? And do you have any contacts there?" Veronica Pilchard was being upstaged yet again by her astute friend but she took it in good humour.

"As a matter of fact I do." Margaret tried not to sound smug. "Let that pig Colliers put that in his pipe and smoke it!" She spat the words out.

"Remind me not to fall out of favour with you Margaret!" Veronica snorted. "Well done! He will get his comeuppance." Veronica Pilchard felt their friendship was on increasingly thin ice.

* * * * *

Nico was unsure how to proceed with the scrap of card from the secret chamber beneath the basement in seven Montague Road. That evening he told Jack about it.

"Ah, now we may be getting somewhere!" Jack was enthusiastic. "Have you touched it? I mean are your fingerprints on it?"

"No. I picked it up with a tissue. Mrs Stock gave me this bag. I thought it might belong to Leo Richards but I am not sure what to do with it."

"It should go to the police – to DCI Emily Brown. She will get forensics onto it." Jack paused. "Could I take a note of the flight number?"

"Sure. Here." Nico opened the bag and Jack noted the details he needed. With the seat and flight numbers and the dates of Nico's incarceration he could check if it was Richards. That would not interfere with the official investigation but it would help his own.

"Now this is in confidence so keep it to yourself, okay?" Nico nodded and Jack went on. "I now know that Leo Richards and another man were involved in an art deal – which may itself be suspect – and we both know Richards was in Eliza's house. The police may get somewhere with this new piece of evidence." Jack wanted Nico to take in the evidence so that he could avoid direct contact with DCI Brown and the possibility of having to lie to her.

Nico agreed to hand in the stub and make a statement to the detectives.

"Now, Nico was there anything else? Was anything strange or out of place that you noticed?" Jack had his investigator's voice on. "Even a small detail might give us a lead."

"Not a thing." Nico mentally retraced his steps during the visit from Mrs Stock. "No, there was something. Someone stole Mrs

Stock's jewellery from the chamber. It's not worth much but it was stolen." He thought on and remembered the MP3 recorder. "There was a recorder in the kitchen cupboard. I put it out of sight as it had a small blood stain and I didn't want Mrs Stock to see it – it might have upset her."

"If that stain is blood then the recorder couldn't have been in the cupboard when the murder was committed." Jack pondered. "It must have been tidied away when the industrial cleaners did their work." Unused to the ways of academics he asked, "Why would Eliza have a recorder? Is that standard for scholars?"

"No. I don't use one. Some people record presentations and lectures instead of taking notes. Maybe that's what she used it for."

Could she have recorded herself for any reason?"

"None that I know of but it's possible." Nico said. "It's odd because she had a more modern recorder. I found it in her office."

"I think it would be worth having a look at what if anything is recorded on both of them – and can you see if she downloaded recordings to her computer?"

"I can try and make time for that tomorrow." Nico was thinking about the work he had to get done on his new home and the amount of time he had to spend with his grandparents. He would make them his priority.

* * * * *

Wild Fern Alley was peaceful. The autumn tidy-up was complete and delicate plants were about to be brought in under glass before the first of the early frosts. The last of the back wall doors was finally painted – at seven Montague Road. The yarn bombing colours were washed and put back in place.

Television cameras and press photographers were recording scenes to be included in features on the City Flowers award. Finally Wild Fern Alley was getting positive publicity untainted by criticisms and allegations from local landlords – who had arranged to meet together that afternoon.

* * * * *

Frederick Stewart was not at the clandestine meeting of the landlords. Cobbles, McVeigh and O'Doherty called themselves the Big Boys club. They sat at a table where they made a habit of meeting – in McVeigh's office, or Poison Corner as Marianne called it - from where the alley and its residents could be secretly viewed. Shappie had heard the news about Stewart's predicament and happily shared it.

"Colliers will go mad! Freddy boy has been questioned by the fraud Squad about fake paintings in his gallery – all of which came from dear Sir John."

"And he spilled his guts I suppose?" Councillor Cobbles was not known for his elegance of speech.

"So I hear." McVeigh was reluctant to reveal the source of this information. Although all four had common cause in opening access to Wild Fern Alley they were bound in mutual distrust in all other matters. "Now O'Property, my man, tell us what you have got for us tonight."

Seamus O'Doherty had been expected to find an official who would do their bidding in the hope of stopping further developments in restoring the missing nineteenth century cobble stones in Wild Fern Alley.

"I came across a guy I was sure we could persuade but he turned out to know that Kelly woman. He said he was going to report me for attempted bribery and corruption." His voice was plaintive and he looked worried.

"That bloody woman! She's a Nazi! She's everywhere and getting people to do all sorts of things – ruining the area." McVeigh spluttered in rage and frustration.

"Maybe we can turn this to our advantage. You say he knows Mrs Kelly. Then we can quietly make it known that she has been unfairly favoured by a friend in the Department." Brendan Cobbles gave a twisted smile of malice.

This was to be a very big mistake as the official in question was a church elder and brother of a senior police officer in the Fraud squad.

McVeigh had his own motives for wanting open access to the alley. He was refurbishing some old flats and completing a wing of new apartments in his unfinished block. He used illegal immigrants for the unskilled labour and persons who wished to remain under the radar for the skilled work. They came and went under cover of darkness and often slept in squalid conditions between long shifts. He paid them badly but fed them well.

Councillor Cobbles had equally venal but different reasons for opposing Wild Herb Alley. He was happy to put up with anti-social activities in the alley so long as he could ferry his own tarts in and out of his latest acquisition – a run-down terrace house which he had bought by gazumping a young family. Rising house prices did not suit any of these landlords – they aimed to buy up property for as little as possible.

That afternoon the good Councillor had to inform his counterparts that he had the duty of presenting the City Flowers award to that Kelly woman.

"Sticks in the throat – and more! I have to do it!" His distaste was genuine but not as strong as he let them think. He might gain from the political leverage and publicity.

Back in Councillor Cobbles' office a young man was writing his speech – noting the importance of this development in the city to the Conservative Catholic Party

* * * * *

Frederick Stewart had told the police all he knew – which did not amount to much. He had known Sir John Colliers for many years and trusted him. Colliers had supplied the paintings and documentation on provenance. He had taken temporary custody of them for the purposes of selling them to some important clients.

He did not know how Sir John had come into possession of the pictures and assured the officer that Sir John was a man in whom one could have faith. "He is President of the Royal Art Society and held in high esteem!" Stewart declared robustly.

The investigating officer did not look at all convinced. "Is that a fact? Well we'll be having a word with Sir John. In the meantime I must have your written agreement that these pictures will not be sold."

With that a somewhat shaken Frederick Stewart was dismissed. He left the station in a state of agitation. He had not had any option but to admit the source of the fake paintings but he knew that Colliers would be furious.

* * * * *

When the police contacted Sir John Colliers he was beyond the point where he could pretend to be cordial. He was red in the face when he answered he front door, clutching a writ in his hand. Cressida's solicitor had served divorce papers that very morning.

Practiced in this procedure Jessica Joyce had knocked on the door, waited for Colliers to appear – knowing him by sight – and confirmed his identity.

"You are Sir John Colliers?" She spoke in a confident and cheerful voice.

"Yes." He replied without the slightest suspicion of what was to come next.

"These papers are for you, Sir John." She handed him an envelope and turned away before he could read the contents. She was driving away by the time he had discovered the writ for divorce.

Shocked beyond the point of reason Colliers sat down on the front doorstep. How could this be? Where was Cressida? Now angered he rose to his feet, went inside and slammed the door shut.

His wife was nowhere to be found. She had taken most of her possessions from her room over the preceding week without him noticing. He could not understand it. Where could she have gone? "That bloody Beightin woman! She will know." He talked out loud as he walked about in an empty house.

It was as he was about to telephone Margaret Beightin that the plain clothes police called.

"We felt you might prefer to speak to us at your home rather than in the station Sir John." Inspector Dunlop spoke in an even non-committal voice.

Unaware of any reason why he police would want to speak to him he invited them in but with less than good grace. "This is not a good time. Tell me how I can help you." Colliers was straining to be civil.

Inspector Dunlop was accompanied by a tall blonde policewoman of at least six feet two. Silent she overshadowed Colliers as he ushered them into the ornately decorated living room.

"We are interested in some paintings that you acquired and were selling through the Stewart Gallery. In particular four pictures – one by John by Luke and three by William Conor." Dunlop noticed a tiny spasm at the corner of Colliers' right eye. He must be nervous. "Can you tell us about their provenance please?"

"I shudder to think that I have been the subject of fraud Inspector." Colliers had made his first mistake. "As President of the RAS I have a reputation you know." His attempts at seeming unconcerned did not hide an underlying anxiety.

"And why would you assume that these works are not genuine?" Dunlop asked with a hint of suspicion evident in his voice.

"Your identity cards show that you are from the Fraud Squad, so I assumed – that's all."

"Might you not just as easily have assumed they were stolen?" The tall blonde DS Riley asked in an even voice.

"Heavens no!" Colliers was affecting a righteous tone. "I had documentation showing the provenance of each painting."

"Sir John you are correct in assuming that we are here about counterfeit – the John Luke and William Conor pieces are not authentic." Dunlop was watching for any other signs of anxiety but Colliers was now cool and collected. "Can you tell me where they came from – that is who sold them to you?"

"With pleasure Inspector! I have been duped – and this will be a huge embarrassment to me." He felt safe in disclosing Richards' name and any details that would deflect police attention away from him. He was calculating that he would not suffer overall loss as long as the Lebrocquy sold. He even considered taking the fake pictures back and passing them on through an auction room in the future. "I bought the pieces from a man called Leo Richards."

The tall blond woman was taking notes, scribbling down details, but also eyeing Dunlop. He was a man who had seen just about every trick in the book when it came to the darker side of the art scene.

Dunlop nodded approvingly "Good, we can follow that up Sir John." He waited for a few seconds and continued. "And how did you meet this Leo Richards?"

Colliers was on unsure ground now, as he had no credible excuse for buying art works from a stranger on the word of Frederick

Stewart. Nevertheless he was angry with Stewart had been happy to put him at the centre of any police suspicions.

"Through the Stewart Gallery as a matter of fact. I have known Frederick Stewart for many years." He said no more, hoping to redirect any doubt away from himself.

"And do you have contact details – for Mr Richards or details concerning your financial transactions?"

Colliers was visibly startled. "Is that really necessary?" He had gone pale and Dunlop decided to give him plenty of rope with which to hang himself.

"I hope not Sir John, but if we have difficulty finding Mr Richards that may be our only means of pursuing the matter." He tried to sound as official as possible, but wanted to leave Colliers without any doubt that the matter would be pursued.

"I can give you the contact details that I have but you might find that Frederick Stewart is better placed to help you. I don't do a lot of administration. Aesthetics is my thing."

Dunlop did not believe a word of it. He was irked that Colliers thought him a fool but simply cleared his throat, shooting a sideways glance at Riley. He wanted to say 'and making a considerable profit' but made do with, "I shall speak to Mr Stewart and if needs be I will get back to you."

The two Fraud Squad officers took their leave politely but without the due respect Sir John Colliers felt appropriate. He couldn't put his finger on it but they were somehow sneering and insubordinate. Colliers was angry. Dunlop and Riley were professionals and shared their observations, agreeing this was going to be a complicated investigation.

Colliers' anger turned to coldness. He must remain above suspicion. Enraged that Cressida had taken into her mind to leave him – thus demeaning his public standing – and mindful of her recently rekindled friendship with Lady Margaret Beightin he calculated that she was somehow the author of both his misfortunes.

He was not aware that Margaret knew it was he who was ringing when she turned off the answer-phone and left the receiver in place.

"Pig!" Margaret muttered under her breath. "Now you will get what you rightly deserve!"

Frustration boiled in Collier's mind. He had to find out where Cressida was and put a stop to her flights of fancy. He would just have to sit it out as regards that interfering Beightin woman – she had too much clout to be brought to heel.

* * * * *

DCI Emily Brown was delighted to meet the handsome young Italian who arrived with instructions from Jack Summers. He had brought evidence that might be relevant to the murder of Eliza Taunter and new information. The theft of Mrs Stock's jewellery was petty but possibly also tied into the murder.

"Thank you Doctor Tebaldi. You may have hit on something very important. I am impressed that you had the presence of mind to avoid getting your fingerprints on this boarding card." She did not add that she was impressed with his solicitous treatment of the elderly Mrs Stock.

She took a liking to this man – more than a liking. She repressed the desire to ask him for a date – being some years his senior – but it was tempting!

He left the police station and spent the rest of the day between his academic duties, visiting his grandparents and starting into renovating a bedroom for them, with the help of an electrician.

Although Nico was busy he eventually did make time to check out the recorders in Eliza's office and kitchen. The more modern one was filled with practice presentations and lectures. It was clear that she like the sound of her own voice – literally. As the human voice is heard by the speaker through his or her jaw bone no-one hears what they actually sound like – and therefore many people don't like the sound of their own voice. Eliza Taunter was one of those rare exceptions. He saved these onto files in a large folder and emailed them to Jack – to his personal email, as requested.

The second, older MP3 model had some similar recordings – some of which were out of date by comparison with the office material but many of which were recent. The last one was strange – and there was so much interference that he was not sure if it was accidentally taken during a television or DVD movie. He could hear Eliza's voice to start off and then it changed – with a shrill female voice screeching at what seemed to be an intruder – then crashing noises, screams and then silence.

He went over this material again, wondering if Jack could get someone more technical to have a listen and took both recorders back to College Road with him.

"I think it might be accidental – like she forgot to switch it off or mistakenly switched it on when she was watching a movie. Even so, since she met such a grisly end you might find it important." Having not heard this last recording until half ten at night he felt he'd been rather selfish – he'd spent the evening working on what was now his home – previously the murder scene.

"Nico I think you should take both the recorders into DCI Brown. Police forensics can probably do a lot with those recordings. Can you do that tomorrow?" Jack tried to sound less than overbearing. "I know you have a lot on. And since I'm on leave I can give you a hand with some of the donkey work – the least I can do when I'm giving you orders about the recordings."

* * * * *

Councillor Cobbles was an inarticulate man preferring bluster to logic. He was barely literate. He was capable of making himself clear but was far from an able orator. So it fell to the party's constituency worker to put together a speech. Marty Miller was a bright and enthusiastic party member who enjoyed writing speeches. He'd been tasked by the party leader, one Manus Simms to put something together that Cobbles could deliver. He sighed thinking to himself that this was some ask!

"Keep the words small – nothing fancy. I'm a plain spoken man." Cobbles instructed.

"Will do." Marty Miller replied, knowing that he could pull out the template for all Conservative Catholic Party speeches – with its emphasis on how high highly the party placed strong family values. "What are the best points about this alley scheme anyway?"

"It is a development which has involved residents in an improvement scheme. It has attracted local media attention and has been assessed as unique by the judges and a model for others to copy." He hated Wild Fern Alley but a presentation of such high profile was something he'd been aiming for all his political career. Although he thought he had blown his chances and particularly with Marianne Kelly, he now had an opportunity to score political points and get a huge amount of positive publicity. Even some national media were due at City Hall. Brendan Cobbles could get to be the next mayor through this exposure!

Marty Miller prepared a gushing speech as an endorsement of Wild Fern Alley and Cobbles read it through gritted teeth. The whole thing was very last minute but extremely important to Miller's future career as well as that of Cobbles. However, as he read the speech it occurred to Miller that 'strong family values' was verging on the homophobic and might need toned down.

* * * * *

Simon and Cal had not been residents for long but were utterly committed multi-taskers, and the soul of diplomacy with outsiders as the residents had started calling anyone but themselves. Backing Thaddeus on all occasions they frequently calmed the volatile Marianne who was increasingly given to verbal excesses in the presence of Cobbles or Shappie in particular.

They were now full committee members and looked forward to the event with some trepidation. Marianne had fulminated with rage when Cobbles name was mentioned.

"That parcel of shit! He is going to present the award?" She railed. "He has done nothing but stir up trouble for us – and those dead rats. You know I have him on camera?"

"Now Marianne. It is the award we all need to think about." Simon spoke in a slow and quiet voice. "Isn't this what you wanted? And he will have to eat his words!" He rubbed his hands and saw Marianne settling down.

"Oh My God! Can you imagine just how much that will gall him?" Cal chimed in.

"True. You have a point!" Marianne almost gurgled at the thought of Cobbles having to sing their praises and endorse their application for a council grant. "I think this might turn out to be an interesting evening."

* * * * *

Detective Inspector Dunlop and Detective Sergeant Riley had enlisted the assistance of the usual Forensic accountant that the police used. Eric Peterson saw through the accounting arrangements immediately.

"This is a fairly standard technique. The practice of moving money from British or Irish banks through overseas companies – going into Swiss bank accounts. Nowadays the Swiss are very cooperative when it comes to criminal investigations. These old methods don't work since the new procedure came in. These people are pretty amateur, although the sums are large enough." He did not ask whether this was a case of tax fraud or the gains of other criminal activity.

"Now I think it's time to call on Sir John Colliers again!" DI Dunlop said.

DS Riley smiled. "Are you going to bring him in?"

"No. Not yet. I have a feeling there is more to this than meets the eye. We can bide our time."

"How can we contact this Peter Saunders boss?" Riley was eager to press on with the case.

"We have an address in the South of France. Once we have interviewed Colliers we can contact the French police. How's your French?"

"Average – I can get by if people speak slowly."

* * * * *

Clive Heedon had intended to endorse Colliers in his bid for National Governor of the BBC. He had made a point of being closely associated with the President of the Royal Arts Society and even courted publicity to lay the ground. Colliers would be useful at some stage he was sure. However, rumours were coming through that Lady Cressida was divorcing him on grounds of domestic violence. The local Sunday rag had all but named Colliers and now, he was reliably informed by Chris Barker, social media was buzzing with the scandal.

"Barker, I think we may have to reconsider this." Heedon pointed to the file on his desk and the draft letter of recommendation. "I don't think this office can be associated with brutality even if it is only rumour at this stage. It could become an embarrassment to us."

Barker noted how Heedon spoke in the plural when it was a matter of some difficulty but always spoke in the first person when the issue reflected well on him.

"That might be a judicious path of action, sir. Shall I dispose of the draft?"

"Yes, thank you Barker." He turned to look out the window over the tree-lined horizon as the civil servant left the room.

* * * * *

Peter Saunders had settled comfortably into his villa and was enjoying the clement weather of the South of France. He was more curious than concerned when he was asked to attend the local police station, thinking it must be connected with the break-in. These country plods had obviously not found anyone.

* * * * *

Jack had checked out the flight details from the boarding card stub that Nico had found – as had DCI Emily Brown. The seat was booked in the name Peter Saunders and he had come by a private company landing in Newtownards airfield. His return had been to the South of France via England. The dates of travel coincided with the murder of Eliza Taunter and the stranger that Veronica Pilchard had seen leaving her house on the morning after her death.

DCI Brown was ahead of Veronica since she had a transcript of the recording which Nico had found on the MP3.

Background noises interrupted a speech or lecture on plurivocity and intertextuality. Eliza sounded alarmed. "Who is it?" a male voice replied, "It's me, Leo."

"No it's not! You are not Leo!" Eliza sounded frightened but also enraged. "What the hell are you doing in my house?"

"It is me Eliza. I have just got a disguise – this is not more hair dye, botox and contact lenses."

"Don't you dare come near me!" She screamed in panic.

"Steady on and put that knife down, Eliza." He sounded impatient. "Don't be so bloody stupid! Arghh! Christ Eliza what have you done?"

The sound of breaking crockery lasted for some seconds, followed by a blood curdling scream, a groaning noise and a gurgling sound. Then silence fell, followed by the male voice saying "Stupid cow – it's your own fault!"

The sounds that followed seemed to be a door closing and a dull moaning and then whimpering.

CDI Brown knew that Leo Richards had disappeared. Now she knew how. He had disguised himself and was presumably now operating under a false identity.

* * * * *

Cressida Colliers stood at the airport waiting for her friend Margaret Beightin who was uncharacteristically late.

Lady Margaret Bieghtin was normally punctual to a fault – so much so that she became very unpleasant with anyone who did her the discourtesy of keeping her waiting beyond the appointed moment that had been agreed. Cressida was worried as she and Margaret had booked a last minute trip to get away from John and his furious pursuit of her. He was enraged that she was suing for divorce and incandescent that news of this had leaked out.

As the call to board the flight came over the public address system Cressida saw a frantic looking Margaret Bieghtin rushing towards the boarding gate.

"Sorry Cressida. There was a bit of a fuss before I got away." She did not go into detail as they were the last to hand in their passes and find a seat.

"Thank goodness you got here in time!"

"Indeed, Pisa here we come!" Lady Margaret Bieghtin grinned. "I will explain when we get settled."

* * * * *

The hunt for Leo Richards now going under the name Peter Saunders produced swift results and would lead to his arrest within a matter of days.

DCI Emily Brown put together the information and hard evidence that she had.

Leo Richards' fingerprints had to be those found in Eliza Taunter's house after the abduction of Nico Tebldi. Richards was now using the name Peter Saunders and could be traced to the Toulouse area. His prints would also be among some of the evidence SOCOs found at the murder scene. If they could access prints from France they should get a match – and this was the first course she took.

Saunders' prints were sent to Belfast from the country plods as he thought of them.

"We've got a hit!" DCO Brown squealed in delight.

Extradition would take a little longer, but the suspect would be in police custody in Toulouse gaol until that was secured.

Peter Saunders' shock was obvious when he arrived at the local station and was charged with murder. He protested his innocence only to be told that the matter would be settled by a British court.

* * * * *

News of Richards' arrest and imminent extradition spread quickly so that the Fraud Squad were given their art fraudster on a plate.

Eager to get out of the murder charge and knowing Colliers and Stewart would ensure as much culpability as possible fell on his shoulders, Richards admitted everything about the fake paintings – but was exonerated as regards the Lebrocquy.

Clive Heedon was too near to Colliers and the local art scene to stick around and resigned as Secretary of State immediately after hearing news of the Fraud Squad collar.

* * * * *

In spite of the landlords' ill-founded allegations and dirty tricks Wild Fern Alley had won the City Flowers award. The committee were due at the presentation in City Hall that evening. Marianne had finally agreed that when Councillor Cobbles presented the trophy she would accept it in good grace. Cobbles had agreed to make the presentation at very short notice when a celebrity television gardener dropped out. It was unfortunate that his trusty phone was not functioning that day as he had an important meeting he needed to cancel but he knew his priority was the media attention and political leverage that would bring.

As Veronica would be in the city centre with Barry Doyle they'd all agreed she'd meet the winning party at the ceremony.

As Councillor Cobbles entered the ball room he looked agitated and looking at his watch but settled at the top table quickly. As a member of the Conservative Catholic Party he was proudly seated beside his wife and the six of his nine children.

It was to be a glittering occasion. Important local and national members of the media were assembled at the back of the room. Around the walls more than twenty tables were elaborately set with sparkling silverware, flowers and candles.

At seven thirty all the invited persons were present at the top table, preening and smiling. Even political opponents were making a show of friendship towards Councillor Cobbles. Large quantities of prosecco were imbibed by all, including guest families, by the time the awards were due to be made.

Despite the fact that she was an important committee member Veronica was late. She arrived just as Councillor Cobbles was about to get to his feet to make the award presentation.

Veronica spotted him at the top table and rushed up smiling and shouting, "Darling Mitchell, I was looking for you, we were supposed to meet at our favourite restaurant this evening to celebrate our six week anniversary! Where were you?"

Councillor Cobbles' wife and six children all look on in horror. Cobbles sputtered, trying to think of some credible explanation but his reddened face and guilty appearance gave him away – to such a degree that it seemed to some that this incident was nothing new. Mrs Cobbles lifted one of the five bunches of flowers destined for the winning team and threw it at her husband – rapidly followed by the contents of a large pitcher of iced water. She cried out "Bastard! Not again!" She hit him across the face as the cameras snapped copious shots, including her striding away from the top table. Her children all cried and followed her out of the ballroom screaming. The committee from Wild Fern Alley had to physically hold back Marianne from joining in the fracas. Cobbles sank into his seat unsure whether to chance proceeding with the presentation. Veronica stared at him with a smug grin.

Rising to his feet Manus Simms, the leader of the Conservative Catholic Party ostentatiously cleared his throat and took the microphone in his hand, "Let me assure you ladies and gentlemen that we are a party of family values and Councillor Cobbles will be standing down as of this evening. I am disgusted at these revelations. As I say we are a party that puts family values first."

"Family values my arse!" A small brunette haired woman shouted from the floor. "I was in a relationship with him and he promised he would leave his wife for me!"

"Hell, no!" A tall blonde woman stood up shouting, "He said the same to me, you tart!" She grabbed the brunette woman by the lapel of her jacket and swung a punch.

A third woman, dressed entirely in emerald green stood up and screamed, "And me – he told me that too!"

As the two other women wrested on the floor the woman in in emerald green lunged at Manus Simms knocking him off balance. Various men started in to defend the blonde and brunette and others just joined in for the fun of the fight. Cameras ran and clicked for the duration of the brawl.

Police entered the ballroom to escort the squabbling parties away.

Order was quickly restored. The committee of Wild Fern Alley insisted that the show went on, which it did in the absence of Cobbles and Danny Wilde. The committee and the press had so much to celebrate!

Veronica Pilchard was not embarrassed. She grinned at the committee. "I said I'd do my bit." She winked mischievously.

"You, Veronica Pilchard, have done us a great service!" Marianne announced to the assembled table. "Manus Simms will be de-selected as leader and Cobbles' days in politics are over!"

* * * * *

The press had their proverbial field day. Pictures on social media went viral. The Barry Doyle Show had an exclusive on the art fraud – carefully avoiding any reference to what turned out to be the accidental death of Professor Eliza Taunter.

Sitting in the Golden Palace the following lunchtime Veronica Pilchard and Barry Doyle were celebrating – the programme had won the Dolby Prize for tell-it-like-it-is journalism.

Barry was in splendid form and lifted a glass of champagne to toast his producer. "Veronica, we have done well. Onwards and upwards! To the next award!" He smiled with unbounded pleasure. "Now I have some other news for you. It will surprise you but it might also explain some things."

He led her down the stairs and out into the back courtyard.

Harry Pilchard in the Golden Palace and in the smoking area! Veronica could hardly believe her eyes.

* * * * *